# "Were yo        make a fool of me?"

Brett's voice was cold. "You called me, then slammed the door in my face."

The suggestion amazed Lisa. "I—called you? Well, I like that!" she flared indignantly. "It was the other way around. It was you who led me to that isolated place. It was you who pulled me down on the sand—your only intention being to use me. But let me tell you this, Brett Arlington, I don't intend to be used in that way." Her voice rang with accusation.

"You're quite wrong, Lisa," he said quietly.

"Oh, in what way am I wrong?" She turned toward him hopefully. Was he about to tell her he'd wanted her because he loved her? If he had, she knew she would have given herself to him. But he said nothing. Apparently the words were not in his mind.

**Miriam MacGregor** began writing under the tuition of a renowned military historian, and produced articles, fiction and nonfiction concerning New Zealand's literary field. She now writes romance novels exclusively and derives great pleasure in offering readers escape from everyday life. She and her husband live on a sheep-and-cattle station near the small town of Waipawa.

## Books by Miriam MacGregor

HARLEQUIN ROMANCE
2710—BOSS OF BRIGHTLANDS
2733—SPRING AT SEVENOAKS

These books may be available at your local bookseller.

Don't miss any of our special offers. Write to us at the following address for information on our newest releases.

Harlequin Reader Service
901 Fuhrmann Blvd., P.O. Box 1397, Buffalo, NY 14240
Canadian address: P.O. Box 603,
Fort Erie, Ont. L2A 9Z9

# Call of the Mountain

## Miriam MacGregor

# Harlequin Books

TORONTO • NEW YORK • LONDON
AMSTERDAM • PARIS • SYDNEY • HAMBURG
STOCKHOLM • ATHENS • TOKYO • MILAN

Original hardcover edition published in 1986
by Mills & Boon Limited

ISBN 0-373-02794-X

Harlequin Romance first edition October 1986

# CHAPTER ONE

IT was a shock to see Paul Mason again. Lisa's blue
eyes widened as a flush crept over the creamy
complexion that complemented her auburn hair. She
stared at him in stunned silence, unable to find words
that would disguise her dismay while questions leapt
about in her mind. What was he doing in the
Arlingtons' lounge?

Catherine Arlington, who had ushered her into the
room, began introductions. Leading her towards a
slim girl with dark hair and soft brown eyes, the older
woman said, 'This is my daughter Mary—well, my
stepdaughter really. Mary, I'd like you to meet Lisa
Longmore. She's come from Auckland with me and
she'll be staying with us for a while. I'm sure you two
girls will become good griends.'

'Yes, of course——' Mary's hesitant tone did
nothing to hide the fact that she was not only
surprised but puzzled as well.

Catherine turned towards the third person in the
room. 'And this is Mary's brother, Brett Arlington.'

Lisa took an involuntary step forward as she found
herself drawn irresistibly towards a tall man whose
hair was almost black and whose dark brown eyes were
mildly curious. He had a firm mouth and chin, and
even if his demeanour was vaguely arrogant he was
one of the most handsome men she had ever seen.

Looking at him, she decided that here was a man
who was determined to do things in his own way. Nor
was she unaware of his magnetic personality which, in
some subtle manner, seemed to breathe an aura of
male strength.

'Did you say—staying with us?' His voice was deep

and vibrant while the glance he sent towards Catherine held a question.

She sighed. 'Yes. It's the book, you understand. I'll explain about it later.' It was then that she led Lisa towards Paul Mason.

But before the introduction could be made the tall sandy-haired man grinned and said, 'How are you, Lisa? It's been a long time.'

She sent him a faint smile but kept her voice steady. 'Yes—three years at least.'

Brett Arlington's voice held a hint of surprise as it cut across the room. 'You've met our neighbour before this evening?'

'Your—*neighbour?*' Lisa was conscious of further shock. Dear God, what had she done in agreeing to come to this place? Were old wounds about to be prised open? No, indeed they were not. She'd overcome the heartache of Paul ages ago.

Recovering herself rapidly, she said, 'I knew Paul when I was doing freelance journalism for the newspaper in New Plymouth, but he wasn't farming in this area at that time, nor in any other area. He was an accountant.' She turned again to Paul. 'I presume this means you *are* farming now?'

'Yes. It was always expected that I'd take over my uncle's property, which happens to be next to this one.'

'It's difficult to think of you as a farmer.' To be honest, she had no wish to think of him in any sense at all.

He gave a slight smirk. 'Oh well, I don't actually break my back over it. I suppose you can call it a type of partnership. Cows, of course, and it's run on a share-milking basis. I own the land, but my share-milker does the work of milking and attending to the herd. We run black and white Friesians, you understand.'

She frowned thoughtfully. 'Yes, I vaguely remember

you once mentioned an uncle who lived towards the southern area of Taranaki. Has he retired?'

'Permanently. He died. He was my father's only brother who lost his wife years ago. There were no children, so he made me his heir,' he added with a satisfied smile.

Lisa became aware that Brett, Mary and Catherine were listening with interest, yet something forced her to pursue the subject. 'It must be a far cry from life in your father's office.'

'Where freedom's concerned, a very far cry. I can now do just as I please. I can drop work to go to the races, to the pub or to the football whenever it suits me.'

She was unable to resist a laugh. 'You haven't changed, Paul!'

The sandy brows drew together. 'What do you mean?'

'Rugby, racing and beer—didn't they always come first?'

'Well, I don't worship at those shrines quite as much as I did,' he conceded gruffly with a quick glance at Mary. 'You mightn't believe it, but I've changed quite a lot.'

'Do any of us ever really change, Paul?' Lisa asked gently.

'Some of us get a little more sense as we grow older—but when it comes to appearances you certainly haven't changed. You're still as lovely as ever.'

She remained unmoved by the compliment. Paul had always been good at flattery, she recalled.

Brett spoke dryly. 'If I may be allowed to get a word in—you two appear to have known each other quite well.'

Lisa turned to face him and was immediately aware of the question lurking within his eyes. Nor was it possible to miss the fact that Mary was regarding Paul with surprise, almost as though she was seeing a new facet to his character. 'Oh, Paul took me out sometimes,' she told Brett casually.

And then Paul came to her aid, almost hastily and as though anxious to change the subject. 'Anyhow, what are you doing here? Have you come for a holiday?'

'No.' Lisa compressed her lips and fell silent. Her reason for being there was Catherine Arlington's business and she had no intention of satisfying Paul's curiosity.

'Even I'm curious about this,' Brett drawled lazily. He turned to his stepmother. 'Come clean, Cathy—you've brought Lisa home for a reason. Something about the book, I think you said.'

She nodded dejectedly. 'Well, yes—it has to be altered.'

'But surely only a little?' Mary ventured to ask.

'A *little*!' Catherine exclaimed wrathfully. 'The whole wretched thing has to be *rewritten*! There are all sorts of things wrong with it, according to my dear brother Gordon. It's too long. It has to be cut down to size, otherwise it's not economic. It's also too regional.'

'What does too regional mean?' Mary asked timidly.

'It means that the interest lies only in the Taranaki district instead of over the whole of New Zealand,' Catherine snapped crossly. 'Really, as he's my own flesh and blood, and as I'm a shareholder in the precious firm, you'd have thought it would have been accepted for publication *at once* and without all these silly quibbles about economics, length and regional interest!' She paused for breath, her hazel eyes flashing with anger.

Brett turned to Lisa, his eyes slightly mocking. 'I presume you'll agree with Gordon.'

'He's my employer,' she replied simply, ignoring the fact that his scrutiny of her face had become penetrating before moving down to her neck. Then, avoiding his eyes, she went on, 'It's also easy for me to understand that it's a matter of sales. Publishing a book costs money, and if it's of interest only in one province the sales will be restricted to that particular district.'

'It sounds as though Gordon's condemned it,' Brett said quietly.

'No, he hasn't actually condemned it,' Lisa hastened to assure him. 'He says it has potential, otherwise I wouldn't be here.'

Brett's eyes ran over her slim form. 'Ah, we're actually coming to the reason for your visit?'

'I have a job to do,' was all she said.

'You've come to rewrite the book?' He gave a sudden laugh that seemed to transform his face. 'Do you know, for one mad moment I wondered if Cathy had brought you home for a totally different reason.'

Catherine glared at him. 'What on earth are you going on about, Brett? Really, you get the oddest ideas!'

'Do I?' He gave another short laugh. 'Okay, so we'll let it rest,' he drawled.

Mary brought the subject back to the book. Looking slightly bewildered, she said to Lisa, 'Do you really intend to rewrite that whole book?'

Lisa hesitated, wondering if Catherine would want the extent of her task discussed within Paul's hearing. Paul, she recalled, was apt to become talkative after the first few pints of beer. How well did these people know him? Was there more than friendship between Paul and Mary?

She turned towards the older woman. 'You've had a long day, Catherine. The journey from Auckland has been tiring, so perhaps it would be better to talk about it in the morning.'

Catherine sighed as she leaned her head against the back of the chair. She closed her eyes which had become shadowed by fatigue, yet even her weariness did nothing to hide the dominance of her nature.

Then, exasperated, she ran fingers through her grey hair that had been carefully rinsed to a deeper hue.

'Oh, what's the use?' she exclaimed, her dejected tones betraying the depth of her disappointment. 'You might as well know the worst. Yes, the whole book has to be rewritten because of its length and—according to Gordon—the amount of trivia that must be cut out.' She paused as the suspicion of a tremor crept into her voice.

Lisa felt a rush of sympathy for her. 'Please don't be too upset about it, but you must understand that its length needs a great deal of pruning.'

'By how much?' Brett's eyes seemed to bore into her own.

'According to the boss—Mr Bishop—the manuscript consists of at least two hundred thousand words or more—'

Mary gave a gasp of amazement. 'Did he *count* them all?'

'No. He took an average of the words on several pages and then multiplied by the number of pages in the manuscript,' Lisa explained. 'He wants me to cut it down to about eighty-five thousand at the most, which is still a fairly large book.'

'You can't do it without ruining it!' Catherine almost wailed. 'It's my life's work——'

'I can only do my best,' Lisa pointed out. 'And you must remember it'll mean the difference between the book seeing the light of day through publication, or spending the rest of its life in the limbo of a bottom drawer.'

'Yes, I understand.' Catherine turned to Brett with further explanation. 'Gordon was keen for me to leave the manuscript with him. He said Lisa could attend to it in her office, but I *pleaded* with him to allow her to come home with me to do the rewriting here at Lynton. I pointed out that by leaving it with him *vital* things could be cut out, and also there'd be numerous things to be discussed during the process. I'm most grateful to Lisa for agreeing to come home with me.'

Brett's mouth twisted into a sardonic smile. 'So that you'll be able to breathe down her neck every time she picks up a red pencil. Isn't that what you had in mind?'

'Well, I'll keep a close watch,' Catherine warned with a veiled glance towards Lisa.

Lisa felt stirrings of unease. Would this task prove to be more difficult than she'd anticipated? Mr Bishop had warned that his sister was a very determined woman, but at the same time he had admitted he was fond of her. He would like to publish her manuscript— but not in its present form.

Paul's voice cut into her thoughts. 'It sounds as if you'll be here for quite a long time,' he observed with a pleased look on his face. 'It'll be good to have you around again.'

Lisa ignored the remark. She was aware that since she had entered the room Paul's eyes had scarcely left her, and the knowledge was making her feel on edge. A tide of weariness swept her and, turning to Catherine, she said, 'If you'll excuse me I'd like to go to bed. I seem to have been in a whirl since this morning.'

Catherine stood up and yawned. 'Of course. I'll make sure you find your way back to your room. You're not the only one longing for bed. Personally, I'm exhausted!'

As Lisa followed her from the lounge she paused at the door to look back and say good night to the others, discovering as she did so that the three people were regarding her with different expressions on their faces. Paul was smirking at her as though confident of intimate tête-à-têtes lying ahead. Mary's face held a trace of concern, while Brett's eyes had become narrowed, his dark brows drawn together in a scowl.

His expression startled her and, vaguely worried as

she wondered if she had offended him in some way, she carried the memory of it as she hurried along the passage after Catherine.

'You should be comfortable in here,' the older woman said as Lisa entered the guestroom. 'You have your own shower, basin and toilet, and these large windows allow the sun to stream into the room. This glass door opens out on to the veranda. I'm glad there are still a few roses blooming in the strip of garden bordering it.'

'Would it be possible to use it as a workroom?' asked Lisa. It would be a retreat, she thought—a place where Paul would hesitate to intrude if he happened to be in the habit of visiting this household.

Catherine was reluctant. 'Brett could put a table near the window,' she said, 'but I can assure you there's much more comfort in the library where a fire burns most of the time. It's May now and the days are cool. Also, my reference books are on the shelves and there could be facts you'd like to check.' She uttered the last words with a light laugh as though the thought of such a possibility was ridiculous.

Lisa made no reply. She knew only too well how easy it was to make errors in a manuscript, and she was also fully aware of the necessity to re-check dates. She crossed the room to stare through the glass door.

Moonlight washed the garden, which was sheltered from the strong westerly winds by a high boxthorn hedge, and beyond it could be seen the rising slopes of Mount Egmont towering to a height of eight thousand, two hundred and sixty feet. Gazing up at the peak that had become cloaked with its early snows, she said, 'Egmont never seems to lose its fascination.'

'Brett would agree with you,' Catherine smiled. 'He adores the mountain and is always clambering up its hidden ways. He's a keen tramper with a great deal of knowledge of the tracks and routes. He belongs to the Search and Rescue Organisation, and of course he skis. He also knows a great deal about the vegetation

on the slopes—in fact one would imagine he owns the
mountain!'

'Or does the mountain own him?' Lisa asked. 'I've
heard it's inclined to get a grip on people.'

'Only if people allow it to,' Catherine pointed out.
'Good night—I hope you sleep well.'

Later, as she lay in the bed that had been
comfortably warmed by its electric blanket, Lisa
reviewed the day's whirlwind events which had placed
her in this position. Had they begun only this
morning? This morning now seemed to be years ago.

It had begun as just an ordinary Friday morning,
she recalled, with a strong and steady breeze stirring
the Waitemata Harbour to choppiness. She had caught
her usual bus on the North Shore, and had gazed at
the numerous yachts as the vehicle had crossed the
Auckland harbour bridge. In the city she had alighted
at the usual stop, had walked along Queen Street
where hundreds of others were hastening to work, and
had been in the office on time.

By morning tea break she had finished editing a
manuscript which had kept her time completely
occupied during the last month. She had sat back with
a sigh of relief and had been about to go to the tea-
room when the head of the firm had walked into her
room.

Gordon Bishop was a large balding man with a
prominent nose and a perpetual frown which, at the
moment, was more pronounced than usual. He had
glanced at the manuscript on Lisa's desk. 'You've
been through it? Do you think it's okay?'

She'd nodded. 'I think it should sell well.'

'Good. I'll have a look at it, then arrange for a
schedule and proof date with the printer. The author
can then do his own proof-reading.' He had then
stared at her, his frown deepening.

Lisa had sensed that all was not well. 'Is something
wrong, Mr Bishop?' she had asked.

'You can say that again!' he had retorted with undisguised irritation. 'I'm wondering if you'll help me.'

'Of course. What can I do?' She had been puzzled.

The rest of their conversation ran through her mind with surprising clarity. It could have been taking place all over again as, lying in the bed, she recalled his words.

'You're aware that this is a family business?'

'Yes.'

'Well, I'm in a spot of family bother. I've got my sister Catherine on my back. You've met her, of course.'

'Oh yes—several times. The last time she was in Auckland we had lunch together at least twice, and we also went to the public library. You gave me time off to help her with research on some of the early Taranaki families.'

'Later she sang your praises because you knew exactly where to find the books she needed. She's taken a real fancy to you.'

'To me?' queried Lisa. 'That's kind of her. I enjoyed helping her.'

'You did? That's fine, because your big chance to help her again is just coming up.'

'I thought you said you wanted me to help *you*,' protested Lisa.

'By helping her you'll be assisting me. You'll get her out of my hair—what there is left of it. The whole trouble is this damned book she's been working on for years.'

'She wants me to go to the library again?'

'A little further than that. She wants you to go home to Taranaki with her.'

'*Taranaki?*' She stared at him in amazement.

'Yes. You'd stay at Lynton, of course. It's a mixed dairy and sheep farm owned by her stepson.'

Lisa continued to look at him blankly. 'I'm afraid I don't understand. You *did* say—Taranaki?'

He sighed and ran a hand over the few hairs on his head. 'I know I'm not being very clear about all this, but the time has now come when she's thrown down her pen and declared the confounded book to be finished. Now she wants the damned thing published—and by us, of course.'

'Naturally,' Lisa agreed with understanding.

'She imagines that because she's a shareholder with a fair-sized interest in the firm—and because I'm her brother—she can just waltz in, plonk the dratted tome on my desk, and I'll do the rest. She can't understand why the size of it sent me reeling backwards. Mind you, I've always known this day would come.'

'And now you're finding difficulty in coping with it?'

'You're dead right, I am! But nor do I want a break with my sister.' Gordon Bishop drew a deep breath, then went on, 'At least she's agreed to have it cut down, but then, in her usual manipulating manner, she's come up with the request for *you* to do it—at Lynton. So—what do you think about it?'

'Is there more than just the cutting down to cope with?'

'Not really. She's called it *Mountain Memory*—the mountain being Egmont. It's really a story of the Taranaki province, Maori wars and all—a history of the people as well as stories about the troubles and trials of the pioneer women. On top of all this there are reams of trivia to be cut out. When I mentioned the word trivia Catherine nearly blew a gasket with suppressed rage!'

Lisa was sympathetic. She knew that dealing with some authors could be tricky, and she could see that in the case of his rather dominant sister Gordon Bishop was having difficulties.

She said, 'I suppose she wants me to do the editing because I've already helped her with a little research—but why does she want me to do it in her home?'

'So that she can keep an eye on the job, of course. She says it'll be better if you're there on the spot because there are sure to be hundreds of queries.'

'She's probably right about that point,' Lisa conceded.

'You could look upon it as a working holiday,' he coaxed.

Lisa was momentarily silenced by the suggestion. What on earth was she agreeing to do? Go back to Taranaki? No, that was the last place in which she wanted to find herself. Yet Catherine needed her assistance, and it was not in Lisa's nature to refuse help where it could be given.

Three years ago when she had come home to Auckland she had been running away from Taranaki. That had been after the affair with Paul Mason, and at that time she had no wish to lay eyes on the province again. Yet heaven knew she longed for another sight of dear old Mount Egmont, with its bush-clad slopes. There was something mystical about that huge peaked heap of extinct volcano with its aura that drew the eyes of all people.

At last she said, 'Where, exactly, is Lynton? Is it near New Plymouth?' She stared at the desk awaiting his answer.

'No, it's a long way out of New Plymouth. It's near Eltham, towards the south-east of the mountain. Does that make a difference?'

'Yes, actually, it does. I'm not keen to work in New Plymouth and I suspect this could turn into quite a lengthy task.'

'It's possible.' His sharp eyes glinted as they bored into hers. 'What's wrong with New Plymouth? Boy-friend trouble at some time?'

'You could say that,' Lisa admitted coolly. 'I've no wish to set eyes on him again—ever.'

'Hmm. Well, you'd better come into my office and talk to Catherine. I'm sure she'll be delighted if you'll agree to go home with her. She's leaving on the five o'clock plane, which doesn't give you much time.'

As they entered Gordon Bishop's office Catherine Arlington put her cup and saucer on the desk. She looked into Lisa's face searchingly as she said, 'Lisa, my dear, you've agreed to come home with me? Gordon said he'd talk to you about it.'

'And in doing so we've both missed our morning tea,' he complained as he pressed a bell to order a fresh pot to be made. Then turning to Lisa, 'Well, what do you say about it?'

She took a deep breath and made a rapid decision. 'Yes, I'll do it.' Somehow the mountain seemed to be calling.

'Oh, I'm so glad!' Catherine exclaimed. 'I knew you'd understand why it's so vital for me to be close at hand while it's being given whatever changes are necessary.' She sent a reproachful glance towards her brother.

'Now you listen to me, Catherine,' he cut in sharply. 'Lisa is an experienced editor. She knows exactly what's needed for a book of this type, she understands what I want and she knows our house style. If you interfere too much by trying to force her to include any of that daft trivia I'll be damned if I'll accept it for publication!'

'Yes, Gordon.' Her tone was deceptively meek.

'Actually I'm being a fool for allowing Lisa to go, because I need her here,' he declared wrathfully. 'And I want her back in this office—do you understand?'

'Of course.' Again there was meekness.

He looked at her suspiciously. 'I trust you haven't any matchmaking ideas in mind—ideas that involve that stepson of yours?'

At the time these last words had barely registered with Lisa, but now the memory of them caused her to sit bolt upright in the bed. *Matchmaking that involved her stepson?* When they'd lunched together Catherine had mentioned a stepson and his sister, but only vaguely because her mind had been almost completely occupied by research for her book.

And what had Brett said this evening? *For one mad moment I wondered if Cathy had brought you home for a totally different reason.* The words had puzzled her, but now their meaning was clear enough. They had meant that Brett also suspected Catherine of matchmaking, and the knowledge made Lisa's cheeks burn. This, no doubt, was the cause of his scowling expression when she had left the room.

Sinking back against the pillows, she recalled Catherine's indignation when her brother had made the suggestion. 'I don't know what you're talking about,' she'd snapped at him.

'Don't you? I think you do,' Gordon Bishop had replied. 'And let me say that if you weren't my sister, and if you didn't have so much cash tied up in this place——'

'You'd see me hopping sideways,' Catherine cut in.

'Well, I suppose we can do this small thing for you,' he conceded reluctantly.

'Thank you, Gordon!' Relief and gratitude appeared to be keeping Catherine's state of meekness to the fore.

After that things had moved rapidly. Lisa had made sure that Catherine was well stocked with typing and carbon paper as well as everything else she considered necessary, and she had then hurried home to pack a suitcase.

When she hurried into the house and announced her intentions her mother had been concerned. 'Isn't this a little sudden, dear?' she had asked anxiously. 'Are you sure you're doing the right thing?'

Lisa had looked at her blankly. 'I don't know, Mother. I only know that something's urging me to go. It's—it's something I have to do. Don't ask me why.'

'Then it won't matter if you come across that Mason fellow again? I must admit I never liked him.'

Lisa had laughed. 'I'm not likely to do that, Mother. He'll be in New Plymouth, whereas I'll be miles away on the other side of Mount Egmont.'

Later her mother had driven her to the Auckland domestic airport where, with Catherine Arlington, she had crossed the tarmac for the five o'clock flight. The plane lifted to curve out over the Tasman Sea, and by the time it banked to land at New Plymouth the last rays of the setting sun were glinting on Egmont's peak.

Catherine's car was collected from a garage where it had been left during her stay in Auckland, and within a short time they were following the main highway southward. Farm homesteads were passed and they sped through the township of Inglewood. Later, when they reached the larger town of Stratford Catherine decided it was time to stop for a meal.

As they got out of the car the chilly air reminded Lisa of her previous days in the province. She had experienced Taranaki's cool winds in New Plymouth when Paul had taken her out a lifetime ago. Thank heaven the memory of him failed to disturb her.

After the meal, and with the mountain always looming on their right, they continued through dairying country until they reached the small town of Eltham where they left the main highway to turn westward.

'We're nearly home,' Catherine had remarked with satisfaction. 'Brett and Mary will be surprised to see me arrive with a visitor. Have I told you about my late husband's son and daughter?'

'No, not really.'

'Brett was fifteen and Mary was ten when I married their father, and that was fifteen years ago, which brings their present ages to thirty and twenty-five. Their mother had died four years previously from a sudden brain haemorrhage. I'm sure you'll all get on well together. Ah, here we are!'

The car turned into a drive where its lights flashed over the dark furry trunks of tall tree-ferns, some leaning out to shelter the way with their umbrella fronds. Lisa caught a brief glimpse of a white timber house frontage before they swung round corners to park at the rear where sheds surrounded a large yard.

Catherine led her in through a back door and along passages to a bedroom. Her case was placed on a small stand, and, having taken off her coat, she was led to the lounge to meet Brett and Mary, who were unaware they had arrived.

And there she had come face to face with Paul Mason.

Even now, lying in the warmth of the bed, she was conscious that the unexpected meeting had left her feeling drained. He looked older, she realised, perhaps because his fair complexion had taken on an outdoor ruggedness, but these changes would be only cosmetic. Beneath the surface he would still be the same pleasure-loving, unreliable, fickle Paul.

Lisa's mind went back to the days in New Plymouth when she had been hurrying about the city in search of news items or feature articles for the newspaper. Her friendship with Paul had ripened to the stage of being serious. At twenty she had found herself peeping at the diamond rings in jewellers' windows, while Paul had vowed she was the only girl he had ever loved. She had believed him and was radiantly happy until one of the older girls at work had taken her aside to utter a warning.

'Lisa, I know it's not my business,' Karen had said, 'but I hope you don't imagine yourself to be the only girl in Paul Mason's life. We've all seen him out with others during the last few weeks. Everyone knows he's a womanising wretch, so don't lose your heart to him.'

'Oh no, Karen, you're quite mistaken,' Lisa had protested.

Karen had looked at her pityingly. 'Surely you know he's been engaged on at least two previous occasions?'

'Perhaps so,' Lisa had smiled, her heart full of understanding. 'But even if it's true it means he will have sown his wild oats and is now ready to settle down.'

'Huh! I know of one wild oat he's having difficulty in keeping underground,' Karen had said scathingly. 'Hven't you met Maggie Simpson yet? She usually waltzes up to him on every possible occasion. I believe she makes a real pest of herself.'

'Who is Maggie Simpson?' Lisa had asked patiently.

'She's a solo mother who does part-time work in one of the motels. I think it's on the waterfront——'

But Lisa had brushed Karen's dark hints from her mind. It was only malicious gossip, she had told herself. Paul was too upright, too honourable to desert a girl who had borne his child. The story was quite ridiculous.

However, a few days later she was having lunch with Paul in a Devon Street restaurant when a girl who appeared to be somewhere near her own age approached their table. Pale and thin, and obviously with little to spend on clothes, she was accompanied by a small boy in his pushchair.

Drawing the child forward, she had given Paul a wan smile. 'Here he is, Paul. He's grown quite a lot since you last saw him, and he's saying more words. People say he's getting more like you every day. He's the spitting image, they say——'

Paul had turned crimson, his eyes glittering with fury. 'What the hell do you want?' he had snarled at the young mother.

The girl had smiled faintly at Lisa. 'I'm afraid it's useless waiting for him to introduce us. I'm Maggie Simpson, and this is little Paul. He's two.'

Lisa had stared at the child's fair hair, light blue eyes and at the unmistakable likeness to the man sitting at the table with her—the man she had thought of marrying. Her bubble of bliss had burst and she had had a sudden longing to go back to Auckland where her parents' home on the North Shore had loomed as a haven of refuge.

But now, after a lapse of three years, she was back in Taranaki. And just along the passage in the lounge of this same house Paul Mason sat chatting complacently. So what? she asked herself with a touch of irritation. So she would just get on with the job she had come to do, and forget he was the neighbour. And if he came to the house she would ignore him.

Her lids fluttered and closed, yet before she fell asleep it wasn't Paul's face that hovered about in her mind—it was the dark-browed image of Brett Arlington, watching her with an expression that could only be regarded as veiled antagonism.

# CHAPTER TWO

WHEN Lisa opened her eyes next morning the vision of Brett's face leapt into her mind, almost as though it had been waiting for her to regain consciousness. The memory of his expression nagged at her, and, pondering over it, she decided it was one of distrust rather than actual antagonism. Obviously there was something about herself that disturbed him, and she came to the conclusion that its cause lay in her reason for coming to Lynton.

However, there was little she could do about it, and as she stood under the warm shower she decided to ignore his attitude; nor would she take more than the barest notice of the man himself. Nevertheless she applied her make-up with extra care, and instead of flinging on a casual blue dress she stepped into one of her more formal office suits. Its green and grey gathered skirt, grey blouse and short green mandarin-collared jacket had the effect of giving her more confidence, which was what she needed at the moment.

A short time later the appetising aroma of sizzling bacon and eggs led her towards the kitchen, where she was given a seat at the breakfast table opposite Mary. Catherine took her place at one end while Brett occupied the head of the table.

He stood up as she walked into the room, his face expressionless. 'You slept well?' he asked politely.

'Perfectly, thank you,' Lisa returned with equal politeness, allowing herself to glance at him only briefly. She then turned to Catherine. 'I've decided to work my normal hours.'

'In that case you'll not be working today,' Brett cut

in suavely. 'Have you forgotten it's Saturday? I doubt that your normal hours include Saturday.' His dark eyes held a mocking glint.

She sent him a level glance. 'Nevertheless I shall make a start on reading the manuscript, which is where I have to begin—no matter what day it is.'

She turned her attention to the food on her plate, still making a determined effort to keep her gaze from the thick black hair, the handsome features and broad shoulders of the man at the head of the table. She had been conscious of them the previous evening, but the shock of meeting Paul again had obliterated almost everything else from her mind.

As though reading her thoughts Mary said quietly, 'I know Paul was surprised to see you—and I think quite pleased, too.'

Lisa had no wish to discuss Paul but hid the fact beneath a casual exterior. 'Really? What makes you imagine he was particularly pleased?'

Mary hesitated. 'Well, he was smiling, so happily.'

'Wasn't that his usual perpetual grin? I seem to recall he was always grinning—like the proverbial Cheshire Cat.'

Brett drawled. 'You and Paul appear to have been old friends.'

'I think I can say I know him fairly well,' Lisa admitted calmly as she met his penetrating gaze. Then, turning to Mary, 'If it's not a rude question, how well do *you* know him?'

Mary flushed. 'He's quite a—a constant visitor—at least he has been lately. We—we like him very much, don't we, Brett?' She turned to gaze at her brother anxiously as though desirous of his confirmation on this point.

'Her blushes tell you everything,' he prevaricated.

Catherine came to Mary's rescue. 'There's nothing to tell.' She turned to Lisa. 'To be honest, we don't know the man very well at all, because it's only during the last few months that his visits have become more regular—although there *have* been times when we've expected him and he's failed to arrive,' she added sharply, as though just recalling this fact.

Brett said, 'Perhaps Lisa knows him better than she cares to admit?' His voice held a question.

Lisa forced herself to give a slight shrug. 'Oh, when I worked in New Plymouth he took me out a few times—and then I went home to Auckland.' She lowered her eyes as she remembered her hasty departure from New Plymouth.

'Why did you go home?' Brett asked quietly.

'Why?' She drew a sharp breath, caught unawares by the query. 'Oh, well, I decided it was time I saw a little more of my parents,' she told him. The wide stare she sent towards the end of the table was steady, and although she was innocent of the fact the green of her jacket reflected in her eyes, making them look like ocean depths beneath cloudy skies.

He returned her gaze without speaking until he stood up abruptly and said, 'I'll see to the library fire. I presume she'll be working in there?' The last words were directed to Catherine.

'Of course—where else?' Catherine returned in a firm voice, and Lisa knew there could be no argument about it. However, Paul had only to set foot inside the room *once*——!

A short time later she entered the small book-lined room to find flames leaping from the pine logs in the open fireplace. Brett was still there, leaning against the mantelpiece as he stared thoughtfully at the glow. He turned to observe her as she prepared for work by placing the manuscript on the table beside a pile of papers on which she would scribble notes.

'It looks as if it'll be a mammoth job,' he remarked, frowning. 'Aren't these editing chores usually done in the publisher's office?'

'As a rule, they are,' she admitted briefly.

'Yet you were able to persuade the powers to allow you to do it here. How did you manage that particular miracle?'

Her eyes flashed as she turned to face him. 'I'm afraid I don't quite understand your meaning. There was no persuading on my part.'

His lips became compressed into a thin line until he said, 'No? I must say your show of surprise at seeing Paul was well played, but I can't help feeling you knew perfectly well he'd be here. Nor were you ignorant of the fact that he's living in the district. Isn't he the *real* reason you wanted to do the job here?'

The accusations made her go dumb for several moments, but at last she managed to say, 'What on earth makes you imagine anything so ludicrous?'

Brett watched her thoughtfully before he said, 'Are you sure it *is* ludicrous?'

'Of course it is,' she snapped furiously. 'Would you mind telling me what gives you this stupid idea?'

'I'm not sure. It's just one of those deep-down convictions. Perhaps it was your utter coolness towards him. It was as though you were being deliberately casual. I mean, if you'd been truly surprised to see him I think you'd have shown it, as well as a little more pleasure in the unexpected meeting.'

'And if the meeting did *not* happen to give me pleasure?'

'As you're old friends, why shouldn't it?' His eyes followed the line of her jaw to her throat. 'Were you lovers?' he demanded abruptly.

Lisa went scarlet, then snapped furiously, 'My oath, you've got a nerve! How *dare* you ask such a question?'

'Well, *were* you?' he persisted calmly.

'No, we were *not*!' she blazed at him. 'Nor is it your business.'

'I'll admit that's true,' he conceded. 'However,

there's the matter of his arrival last evening. During the afternoon he told Mary he wouldn't be seeing her, and then, lo and behold, he turns up after all, a bundle of borrowed agricultural magazines beneath his arm. It was almost as though he'd been given the message that you'd be here.'

Lisa was incredulous. 'Surely you're not suggesting that I phoned him?'

His mouth twisted. 'Yes—unless somebody else did so.'

The dark eyes were so penetrating she almost quailed beneath their glare until curiosity made her ask, 'What makes you so sure he received a phone call? Did he say so?'

'No—but it seems logical.'

She took a deep breath to control her anger. 'In other words you're accusing me of using this place and Catherine's book as a means of enabling me to see Paul Mason?'

'It's possible, isn't it?' His eyes held accusation.

She met their disapproval steadily. 'It's possible, but most improbable. But even if it happened to be true—which it *isn't*—why should it worry you?'

'Because it'll hurt Mary. She appears to have fallen in love at last, and I don't want to see a spanner thrown into the works.'

Lisa gave a short laugh. 'Rest assured, I don't carry spanners, nor have I any intention of hurting Mary. Now if you'll excuse me I'd like to get to work.' She sat at the table, opened the manuscript and stared almost unseeingly at the first page.

But despite her efforts concentration eluded her. Vitally conscious of the man, she realised his resentment towards herself was a double-edged sword with enough cutting power to disturb her. Firstly, he had suspected she was being thrown at him in a matchmaking project, and secondly he was sure she had wormed her way into his household because of Paul.

In an attempt to shut these thoughts from her mind she concentrated on the manuscript's title: *Mountain Memory*. It was most appropriate. Previously that same mountain had had the power to bring back memories of Paul, and now he himself had returned to plague her.

She shook herself mentally, realising that he would plague her only if she allowed him to do so—and for Pete's sake, why was she facing the possibility before it had even raised its head? In doing so she was creating obstacles before they'd occurred.

Following the first few pages of closely packed narrative, she learnt of conditions in England's south and west counties during the previous century, and of the hunger and poverty which had made the people of Devon and Cornwall consider emigrating to a country on the other side of the world. The opportunity for them to take this giant step had come when a newly formed body calling itself the Plymouth Company was launched at a public meeting in Plymouth in the January of 1840.

Lisa read several pages of details concerning its directors, then became aware that Brett was still in the room. She knew that he watched her intently and she made a determined effort to ignore him. Even so her neck felt hot as a flush began to steal upwards.

At last he spoke. 'Well, how does it read?' he drawled.

Her brows rose. 'You should know. Or haven't you read it?' she prevaricated, having no wish to tell him she found the opening to be dry and slow, the paragraphs too lengthy.

'I've glanced at it,' he admitted. 'Perhaps I've heard too much about it over too long a period. Anyhow, it's not my cup of tea.'

'You were bored?' she asked quietly.

'Indescribably.'

'Then we'll have to see what we can do to raise and

hold your interest,' she replied, keeping her voice even.

He gave a sardonic laugh. 'You'll have to work damned hard to do that!' Then, surprisingly, his tone change to a softer note as he added, 'By raising my interest you wouldn't be referring to something other than the book, by any chance?'

She turned and met the long penetrating stare from the dark eyes. 'Whatever can you be going on about, Mr Arlington? As far as the book is concerned I can only do my best.'

Her eyes returned to where several pages described the many attractions of the new land. There would be no winter as they knew it, the prospective emigrants were promised. The fertility of the soil was such that crops would spring up from the ground almost before the planters had turned their backs—indeed, it would be almost necessary to jump out of the way.

Lisa laughed as she read the last few lines.

'Don't tell me you've struck a patch of humour in it,' Brett remarked ironically. 'Humour was never Catherine's forte.'

She sat back and looked at him. 'Are you always sarcastic about the efforts other people make, or is it just that you're annoyed because I'm here?'

'Of course I appreciate effort,' he snapped, then lapsed into a moody silence.

'Then you must be irritated because I'm here,' she accused, looking at him unflinchingly as she awaited his denial.

But it did not come, and he merely glowered at her for several moments before leaving the library.

She returned to the manuscript, acutely conscious that for some reason the room had taken on a feeling of emptiness. He had disturbed her while he had been *in* the room, surely he couldn't disturb her while he was *out* of it?

The next person to break into her reading was

Mary, who brought in coffee at mid-morning. 'Aren't you bored with all that old stuff about the early settlers?' she asked, nodding towards the manuscript. 'I tried to read it, but I'll admit I'd rather have a romance any day.' She placed the tray on the table. 'Anyhow, Brett says you're allowed to work this morning, but not this afternoon.'

Lisa sat back and sipped the steaming beverage. '*Brett* says? He intends to dictate my hours?'

'It's Saturday. He says you don't normally go to the office on Saturday, so you'll be coming with us to the rugby match in Hawera. We'll be leaving after lunch.'

'I'm afraid I'm not really a rugby fan,' Lisa demurred.

'But Brett says it's all arranged, so you'll be coming with us.'

Lisa bristled inwardly. 'Am I to take it that Brett arranges the activities of everyone in this house?

'No, but he says it's all fixed. He phoned Paul and we're to meet him near the entrance gates.'

'Paul? He'll be with us?' Lisa's heart sank.

Mary nodded, her soft brown eyes widening a little apprehensively as she looked at Lisa. 'You'd—you'd like Paul to be there, wouldn't you?' Her tone was anxious.

'Not particularly. Why should I want him to be there?'

'Because—well, I just thought——'

'Yes? You just thought what?' Lisa demanded.

'Didn't you come here because you knew he'd be next door?'

'Definitely not. Is that what Brett told you?' she asked sharply. 'If so, he's entirely mistaken.'

'He—he said he was wondering about it.'

'Then he can stop wondering—and the sooner the better! Please believe me, Mary. I want you to understand that I had no idea Paul would be living in the vicinity of this place, for the simple reason I've had no communication with him for three years.'

Mary's spirits appeared to lift as a flush stole into her cheeks. 'You really haven't? I do want to believe you.'

'Then let me assure you I haven't spoken to him since I left New Plymouth and went home to Auckland. I'll admit he wrote a couple of letters which I refused to answer—and I also recall he once told me he had an uncle who was farming towards the south of Taranaki, but the exact locality of the property was never mentioned. So if you're enjoying a special friendship with Paul you have nothing to fear from me.'

Mary's flush deepened. 'I'm—I'm so very glad,' she said quietly. 'To be honest I—I was afraid.'

Lisa looked at her searchingly. 'I know it's not my business, but—is there a definite commitment between you and Paul Mason?'

Mary's eyes clouded a little as she shook her head. 'No, not yet, but I'm hoping there'll be one quite soon.'

Lisa was filled with compassion as she grasped the situation. Dear Heaven, she thought, where Paul was concerned Mary was in the same position as she herself had been, but what could she say or do about a situation which, after all, was neither her problem nor her business? As she pondered the question the old proverb about a still tongue making a wise head leapt into her mind, yet at the same time she had a strong conviction that she should say something. It was only fair that Mary should be warned that Paul was not the most reliable man in the world. Or had he changed? She doubted it.

'Brett and Paul are close friends?' she asked, watching Mary from across the top of her coffee mug.

'Oh no, Brett has very little contact with Paul because every minute of his spare time is spent on the mountain. Also, as Paul has been our neighbour for such a short time Brett hardly knows him.'

'Are you saying that Brett hasn't bothered to become friendly with Paul?'

Mary hesitated, then admitted reluctantly. 'When they first met Brett didn't like him at all, but I've tried to persuade him to *try* to like him—for my sake.'

'Do you think you've succeeded?'

Mary sighed. 'I don't know. We've been to a few rugby matches together, but I'm afraid Brett doesn't really like Paul's attitude. He becomes so excited when the local team is winning, and so mad with rage when they're losing. His attitude doesn't annoy me—it just makes me laugh.'

Lisa gave a small shrug. 'It won't matter to me if he dances on the grandstand roof with his hair on fire—I won't be there to see it. I couldn't care less about rugby matches, and what's more I intend to stay home and get on with the job of reading this manuscript.'

Brett's deep voice came from the doorway. 'Is that a fact? Nevertheless you'll put on warm clothing and come out for some fresh air.' The log he threw on the fire sent the flames leaping. 'There now, that should last until lunchtime when I'll rebuild it because Catherine has decided to write letters this afternoon. I've told her you're coming to the football with us.'

Lisa faced him squarely, conscious of the quiet determination behind his words. 'Are you insisting that I come against my will?'

'You can put it that way if you like,' he drawled. 'Mary usually wears a warm track-suit. Do you happen to possess such a garment? If not I'm sure she'll have a spare one to lend you.'

'I have my own track-suit, thank you,' she found herself saying, knowing that despite her claim of preference to remain in the library she would be with them at the match.

After lunch she took it from her case and as she

pulled up the front zip of the jacket the royal blue colour turned her eyes to deepest delphinium. Mary wore a similar garment in tan, and both girls added matching caps and gloves. By that time Lisa was aware of an inner excitement she found difficult to suppress, but not even to herself would she admit that it had anything to do with the fact that she was going out with Brett Arlington.

When his silver-grey Holden drew up at the door she moved to take a seat at the back, but he forestalled her by opening the door to the front passenger seat, indicating that she should sit beside him. She turned apologetically to Mary, fearing she was usurping her place, but the suggestion was waved aside.

'It's obvious Brett wants you in front with him,' said Mary as she climbed into the back seat. 'I wouldn't dare argue about it.'

As the car cruised along the undulating road towards Eltham Lisa tried to relax, but found herself becoming increasingly aware of the man sitting beside her. In an effort to drag her mind away from him she gazed through the windows and concentrated upon the scenery. Behind them the mountain rose in majesty like a wide inverted cone, the snows on its peak not yet down to the bushline.

Closer at hand and on either side of the road, the land was divided by prickly hedgerows of light green boxthorn, the low shelterbelts being so typical of the Taranaki landscape. Some of the fields were grazed by sheep, others by herds of Jersey or black and white Holstein milking cows.

Eltham was approached, and as they drove through its short main street Brett remarked casually, 'I suppose Paul has told you that this small town is famous for its cheese-making?'

Lisa turned to look at his profile, noting the straight nose and chiselled mouth. 'I don't recall Paul being particularly interested in cheese,' she remarked lightly.

'However, almost every Taranaki schoolgirl knows that Eltham is famous for its tasty blue-veined variety.'

He frowned as he stared straight ahead. 'Are you saying Paul hasn't told you about his interests in the manufacture and exporting of butter and cheese?'

'Good heavens, no. Why should he tell me these things? Three years ago he wasn't even remotely interested in such commodities—apart from eating them, of course.'

'Strange. Very strange.' Brett's tone held a note of disbelief.

Lisa looked at him wonderingly, then decided to be frank. 'I have a strong feeling you're trying to trap me into an admission of some sort.'

'Oh——?' His tone was noncommittal.

Irritated, she went on, 'You appear to imagine I've been in constant touch with him. I've told you, it's three years since I last saw him in New Plymouth.'

'And letters haven't passed between you?' He glanced at her mockingly, then turned again to the road ahead.

'No, they have not!' she snapped angrily.

He gave a short laugh before remarking dryly, 'In any case I doubt that dairy products would hold first priority as the subject of letters. I'm sure they'd be much more personal.'

'Why are you so determined to link me with Paul Mason?' she demanded furiously, a flush staining her cheeks. 'You're being insufferable about something that's not your business. Is this why you insisted I sat in front with you—so that you could cross-examine me?'

'I'm just assessing the situation,' he returned easily.

'The *situation*—what on earth are you talking about?' She fell silent as sudden enlightenment dawned upon her. Any emotional situation between Paul and herself would naturally affect the romance

budding between Paul and Mary—and, as she had
already guessed, herein lay one of the reasons for
Brett's underlying resentment towards herself.

So far he had not admitted to it openly, but she
could sense it was there, and the knowledge niggled
until it hurt like a nagging ache. Nor did she enquire
too closely as to why this should be. Brett had done
nothing to endear himself or offer any charm towards
her—quite the opposite, in fact—yet she felt drawn
towards him. She was being a fool, she told herself
sharply.

The silence between them became strained until
Mary spoke to Lisa from the back seat. 'Has Brett told
you about Chew Chong?' she asked.

Lisa grasped at the change of subject. 'No. Who is
Chew Chong?'

'He was a Chinese merchant who traded in Eltham
during the early settlement days.'

'She'll read about him in Catherine's book,' Brett
pointed out.

'Tell me about him,' urged Lisa, anxious to avoid
another long silence in the car.

'He was a most enterprising man,' Mary told her.
'While travelling about Taranaki he noticed large
quantities of fungus known as Jew's ear growing on
burnt or decaying logs. He discovered it to be edible,
and recognised it as being similar to a Chinese plant
which was highly prized as a delicacy, as well as being
used for medicinal purposes——'

Brett cut in, 'Chew Chong offered to buy all that
could be collected, so the wives and children went out
to gather it. They packed it in flax baskets and took it
to Chew Chong who exported it to China. It became
known as 'Taranaki wool' because the district was
developing as cow country rather than as sheep
country.'

'I was telling the story, Brett,' Mary reproached
him wrathfully and in an aggrieved voice.

'You'd be wiser to think of stories to tell Paul,' he teased. 'Let him see you're not a complete mouse.'

'But don't take too seriously the stories Paul tells you,' Lisa advised gently.

Brett sent her a glance through narrowed lids. 'What's he likely to tell that she mustn't believe? Something about you, perhaps?' he added softly.

She ignored his last words. 'He could try to make her believe she's the only girl in the world for him—— '

'Is that what he told you?' Brett murmured.

'—but only time will prove whether or not this is true.' She turned impulsively towards the back seat. 'Please be warned, Mary.'

For a moment she feared her words might have upset Mary, but this did not appear to be the case. Instead of wearing a stricken look Mary was smiling, her eyes full of confidence. It was as though she was sure Paul loved her and was merely waiting for the right moment to ask her to marry him.

Lisa sighed and turned to the front again, then realised the car was running along the last straight towards the built-up area of Hawera where another meeting with Paul was at hand. She told herself she was worrying unduly, and that if she was to complete the editing of Catherine's book she would have to become accustomed to the sight of him. At least she could always escape to the library—or so she hoped.

Brett parked the car in a side street, then they made their way towards the rugby grounds where they found Paul waiting among the crowd near the gate. He greeted them cheerfully.

'Hi there—I've bought the tickets, so we can go straight in.' He threw an arm round each of the two girls and planted a kiss first on Lisa and then on Mary.

Lisa noticed the action was not lost on Brett, whose eyes suddenly narrowed to slits as they stared accusingly at her. Her cheeks flamed as she wrenched herself away from Paul's grip.

But Mary did not appear to resent Paul's attention towards Lisa, possibly because she felt sure that she herself came first with him. Her face glowed and her eyes shone as she gazed up at the tall fair man. 'Oh, thank you, Paul, that was thoughtful of you,' she said happily, 'but I know Brett will insist on paying for our tickets.'

'Like hell he will!' Paul declared with much show of generosity. 'Let's go and find seats on the stand.' He tucked Mary's hand beneath his arm, and as they followed the crowd towards the grandstand he also made an attempt to take Lisa's arm.

She snatched it away angrily. 'Please keep your hands off me!' she muttered as she moved away from him.

'What's the matter with you?' he demanded peevishly. 'I've taken your arm before today, haven't I?'

'That's right,' she agreed. 'But the last time you did was definitely the *last* time. Do you understand?'

'No, I'm damned if I do. What the devil's wrong with you, Lisa? You used to be so nice to me.'

'That was before I woke up,' she snapped with some heat. Brett walked beside her as they moved towards the stand. 'Quite a show of indignation,' he remarked with what sounded like forced affability. 'It's for Mary's benefit, I presume.'

'You may presume as you wish,' Lisa retorted coldly.

'Relax and enjoy yourself.' His voice held a note of command, then, pointing up into the stand, he said, 'Look, there are four empty seats about midway up.'

To her surprise he took her hand, almost dragging her up the steps between the tiered rows. The firmness of his grip sent tingles racing through her nervous system, making her catch her breath, and as they reached the row with the empty seats there was a pause while his gaze held her own. It was almost as though an unspoken message passed between them, but suddenly the spell was broken as he dropped her hand and led her along the row.

'I trust you won't object to sitting beside me—or would you prefer to sit beside Paul?' he asked sardonically.

'Don't be stupid!' she snapped, disappointed because his words had extinguished the faint spark that, for one brief moment, had flickered between them.

Kick-off time came a few minutes later, the crowd cheering lustily as both teams in their different coloured jerseys ran out on to the field. Then came two separate periods of play when the home team did its best to vanquish the visiting fifteen men from another district.

Excitement ran high as players raced down the field passing the ball from one to the other, with crescendoes of angry criticism being roared at anyone who dared to drop it. Bellows of fury greeted referee decisions that failed to satisfy the crowd, while cheers shook the grandstand as goals were kicked.

Lisa noticed that Brett's reaction to the game was controlled. She knew he became tense at critical moments when the ball was near the opposition's goal line, but he also applauded their good play.

In contrast Paul was completely uninhibited, and as his emotions fluctuated between approval or disapproval of the performance on the field he seemed to lose all control. He shouted and yelled with delight when the game pleased him, or fumed like a petulant child when it failed to go the home team's way.

She glanced at Mary, who was sitting beside her. 'Brett and Paul enjoy the game very differently,' she whispered.

Mary looked blank. 'Oh? Do they? In what way?'

'Well, it's easy to see that Brett feels for the other

side as well as his own side. He appreciates good play on their part. He's a true sportsman.'

'Are you saying Paul isn't a good sport?' whispered Mary with a flash of indignation.

Lisa shrugged and said nothing, realising that Mary was so obsessed with Paul she was unable to see him clearly.

Later, as they were leaving the grounds, Paul was in a good humour after the home team's win. Mary smiled at him and said,

'You'll come home with us for evening meal, Paul?'

He sent a quick glance towards Lisa before replying to Mary's invitation. 'Thank you, but I'm afraid not. I have a prior engagement—one that's quite important.'

'Oh.' Mary's face fell, betraying her disappointment.

Lisa looked at him steadily. 'Those words have a familiar ring about them, Paul. I seem to have heard them before.'

He grinned at her. 'You have? I'm afraid I don't know what you're talking about.' Then after a hasty glance at his watch, 'I'd better be off—it's later than I thought. No doubt I'll see you some time next week,' he promised Mary.

'Can't you come tomorrow?' The brown eyes were pleading.

He looked at her, almost as though taking pity. 'Well, yes, perhaps I'll see you tomorrow.'

As they watched Paul stride towards his car Brett swung round to face Lisa. 'That was an odd thing for you to say. Why should a prior important engagement sound familiar if, as you claim, you've neither seen nor heard of him for three years?'

'Because it was——' The words died on her lips as she glanced at Mary's expression, which still reflected disappointment. A wave of sympathy swept her, making her feel that now was not the time to explain that this was the excuse Paul had used on various occasions in New Plymouth. It was easy to see that Mary was unhappy, and as Lisa had no desire to heap coals on the embers of her depression she told Brett firmly, 'If you don't mind, I'd prefer to leave the subject alone.'

Little was said on the way home, and although Brett did not press Lisa for further explanation she had a strong feeling he was annoyed with her. So to escape more questioning she made her way to the library as soon as they reached the Lynton homestead. Catherine had finished her letters and was no longer using the room, but even with the book-lined walls to herself she found difficulty in concentrating on the manuscript.

At last she left the table, opened the French doors and stepped out on to the veranda to gaze at the outlined symmetry of the mountain. The sky beyond it was washed with the deepest pink of evening, while the sun's last rays threw a kaleidoscope of crimson, gold and mauve into the long wisps of clouds drifting from the summit. Sighing, Lisa mused aloud, 'You fascinating great pile, when did you last blow your top?'

Brett's voice spoke unexpectedly from behind her. 'Geologists believe the last eruption occurred almost four hundred years ago.'

She swung round to face him and was startled by the intensity of the expression in his eyes. Had he come to question her further about Paul? In an effort to keep him from that particular subject she sent her gaze skyward and said, 'The clouds are so beautiful.'

He crossed the room to stand beside her. 'When they drift eastward it's said he's sending his love back to Pihanga. You know the old legend, I suppose?' Surprisingly, his voice had softened.

'Of course. One can't live in Taranaki without learning of it sooner or later. According to the ancient Maoris he once stood with the group of mountains south of Lake Taupo. Apparently he fell in love with Mount Pihanga, the wife of Mount Tongariro, and there was a mighty battle, until Taranaki was vanquished and fled to where he now stands.'

Brett nodded. 'That's right. To the early Maoris he was always known as Taranaki until Captain James Cook explored along the coast and renamed him Egmont after England's First Lord of the Admiralty.'

Lisa pursued the subject which kept them from speaking of Paul. 'I recall being told that during earlier days not a single Maori would live in the direct line between Taranaki and Pihanga.'

'That was because many of them believed the day would come when he'd uproot himself and return to his loved one, and it was also feared that Pihanga might do the same. They knew that if Pihanga had been a human instead of a mountain she would have gone searching for him. She would have tramped through the dense bush, scrambling up hills and slithering down steep gullies for miles on end to find him.' He paused and there was a brief silence before he added with a slight edge to his voice, 'Today she can do it so much more easily, reaching any part of the country by plane or by car.'

Lisa caught her breath, then became very still before she said, 'Do I detect a personal attack, Mr Arlington? It's obvious you're determined to believe I came here searching for Paul.'

'If you want the truth I believe you must have heard he was living near your boss's sister—so, when the opportunity came for you to edit her book here, you snatched at it with both hands.'

The idea was so far from reality she was unsure whether to laugh it away or to allow him to become aware of the anger that was beginning to bubble within her. At the same time she didn't want to quarrel openly with him because the resulting antagonism might put her into a state of being unable to do her work well. At last a forced smile played about her lips as she said, 'Now I know why you were so determined that I should accompany you to the rugby match—and why you arranged for a foursome.'

Brett looked at her sharply. 'You do? I'd be interested to know what your imagination declares my reasons to have been.'

'Not imagination but fact,' she snapped. 'You wanted to watch us together. You were anxious to observe Paul's reactions to me—to say nothing of my reactions to him. It's as simple as that. I'm sorry if you drew a blank despite your carefully laid plan.'

The cold anger in his face was enough to confirm that her accusation had been correct, while the sudden laugh she was unable to suppress only served to bring the dark brows together in a scowl. For a moment she feared he was about to grab her by the shoulders and give her a good shaking, but he turned on his heel and left the room.

# CHAPTER THREE

THE abruptness of Brett's departure had a sobering effect that put an end to Lisa's amusement, while the knowledge that she had really angered him disturbed her to the extent of making concentration impossible; therefore, instead of returning to the table she remained at the French doors, staring towards the mountain yet seeing nothing.

The situation was obvious, she realised. Brett was positive she had come to find Paul, but despite her denial it was plain he had decided she was lying. Nor was it likely he would ever believe her, no matter how much she tried to convince him that such was not the case.

'Very well, Brett Arlington,' she muttered quietly to herself, 'you can believe as you please. What do I care? Catherine's book is my first priority, and the moment it's finished I'll be away from this place like a homing pigeon.'

But for some unknown reason she knew she *did* care—and although she went to sit at the table to make a determined effort to work the words on the pages hardly registered. At last she told herself she was tired after the tensions of the last few hours, and apart from that fact it was Saturday, which was normally a holiday for her.

The latter thought was enough to make her push the manuscript back into its folder, and after a few restless paces about the room she found herself back at the French doors, where, leaning against the frame, she tried to shrug off the cloak of depression that was beginning to wrap itself about her.

But a few moments later tension gripped her again

as sounds from behind indicated that Brett had returned to the room. Determined to keep her back to him, she knew he poked at the logs on the fire, and when he joined her at the open door she still tried to ignore him.

However, to ignore Brett Arlington was an impossibility as, despite her former intentions, her face was drawn towards him by an invisible magnet. She was then startled to discover his eyes to be slightly narrowed as they rested upon her.

'Okay, so I did want to observe you and Paul together,' he admitted at last. 'Surely you can understand that my concern is for Mary?' He stared moodily towards the mountain. 'I wish I knew whether she really loves Paul, or whether she's grasping at the chance of a marriage that will keep her in the district and close to Catherine and myself. She's a mouse, and we're her security.'

'Then it's high time she got out of the district and saw a little of the world for herself,' Lisa snapped crisply. 'Girls who spend their lives in country areas have little chance of meeting desirable men. Can't you see that for yourself? It's my guess that Mary's led an isolated existence. She might as well be married to old Taranaki himself for all the life she sees——'

'It would bore you to live here for the rest of your life?' he asked in quiet tones.

'Not at all, as long as it was with a man I love.'

'With Paul, for instance?'

She swung round to face him, fury raising sparks that turned her eyes to blue diamonds as she almost shouted at him, 'No, not with Paul! How can I get it through to you that I did *not* come here looking for Paul? Granted, we had an affair three years ago—but that also *ended* three years ago.' Frustration made her want to scream, and it was an effort to keep herself under control.

'That's the truth?' he demanded quietly.

'Of course it's the truth. Why can't you believe me?' Lisa's voice shook slightly.

'Very well, I'll try.'

'Then let me warn you, if Mary marries Paul she's more than likely to rue the day. I'm amazed to see you encourage the match.'

'I do so only because he appears to be Mary's choice. To be honest, I hardly know him, because we've little in common, but I don't want to interfere if she's sure her happiness lies with Paul. She considers him to be a decent chap.'

'According to his own lights he's a very decent chap,' Lisa snapped, then added bitterly, 'But he's unstable. One woman is not enough for him.'

'That was your experience with him—the cause of the break-up between you?' Brett was watching her closely.

'Yes—but I don't intend to talk about it.' She left him abruptly and went to the fireplace, where she stood staring down into the flames, furious with herself for having almost lost her temper.

The sound of his footsteps told her he had followed her across the room, and although she knew he now stood behind her she did not turn round. Then, startled, she caught her breath as she felt his arms about her as firm movements turned her to face him.

His finger beneath her chin raised her face while he looked down into her eyes. 'And what about you, Lisa Longmore? Would one man be sufficient for you?'

'Of course. How dare you suggest otherwise?' Her face flamed as she glared at him, and although she tried to shrug his arms from about her body their grip tightened, sending quivers down her spine and causing her pulses to race.

'Tell me, what would you ask of that one man?' he demanded.

Lisa knew her heart was thudding and wondered if he was aware of it. Nevertheless she managed to meet his eyes defiantly as she replied, 'No more than the average woman would ask of any man. Love, tenderness, fidelity. Yes, definitely fidelity.'

In the gloom of the shadowed library his face looked pale against the darkness of his hair, while his eyes appeared to be black except for where they caught a spark of red light from the fire. He lowered his head, and as she gazed up at him in a state of hypnotic immobility his firm mouth came down to find her own in a kiss that was possessive.

The action sent a shock tingling through her nerves, but even as she told herself to keep her head and resist his embrace her soft lips parted, while she found herself responding to the dangerous teasing of his mouth. Nor was she unaware of the gentle kneading of his strong fingers as they explored the muscles of her back.

Seemingly of their own volition her arms wound themselves about his neck, while her fingers fondled the crisp dark hair curling above the polo collar of his sweater. The action was enough to admit her response, and his clasp tightened to mould her to the male contours of his body. Then, as his hands glided from the small of her back to press her thighs even closer to his own, his kiss became more intense as it sent its message of deeper demands.

He's being nice to me, Lisa thought wildly. It's—it's almost as though he's longing to make love. Why is he being so nice?

It was then that a wave of common sense swept through her chaotic mind and brought her down to earth as she recalled the accusations Brett had previously levelled at her—accusations which amounted to a barrier of distrust. He had been so bitter and suspicious, but now there appeared to be a complete turn-about on his part. *Why*, for heaven's sake?

It wasn't because he was in love with her, that was

for sure. How could he be on such short acquaintance? Could it be that he was merely testing her reaction to another man's caresses? If so it meant that he didn't really believe in her immunity to Paul's attentions.

The jumble of questions continued to dart through her mind until she felt thoroughly bewildered. A sense of shame at having found herself so susceptible to Brett's magnetic personality engulfed her, and, suddenly infuriated, she wrenched her mouth from his. Her hands found their way to push against his chest while she struggled from his grasp, then fled to her room, where she paused to lean against the closed door.

At last she stirred herself to cross the room and gaze into the mirror. Her blue eyes, fringed by their dark lashes, were shadowed by anxiety as she still pondered the question of why Brett should kiss her with such ardour. Was it sheer male dominance—a warning that he would take what he wanted when he was ready to do so? Or was this the pretence of an affair that would lead to nowhere and merely keep him amused while she edited Catherine's manuscript?

At the same time the memory of his demanding kiss as his arms crushed her against his body caused her to flush as her breath quickened, and in an attempt to calm her jangled nerves she straightened her back, picked up her brush and applied strong vigorous strokes to her dark auburn hair.

'Oh no, you don't, Brett Arlington!' she muttered fiercely to herself. 'You can't fool me with those phoney kisses. I can see through your little game!'

So what attitude should she take? Ignore it, she resolved. Treat it as though it had never happened. And with this decision fixed in her mind she set about changing from her track-suit to an attractive dress of fine dark red wool that sent a glow to her cheeks. The skirt hugged her slim hips before swinging out in a flare of pleats, while the bodice, moulding her rounded breasts, was cut low enough to reveal a hint of cleavage.

Her reason for putting on what was literally one of her best dresses was something she avoided asking herself, nor did she pause to wonder why she paid so much attention to her make-up. However, as the final smoothing of colour was giving Lisa's lips an inviting gleam, Catherine came into the room.

The older woman stared at her with undisguised admiration. 'My goodness, you *do* look nice,' she declared with sincerity. 'That's a most attractive dress—it gives you warmth.'

'Yes, it's wool,' said Lisa, deliberately misunderstanding.

'I didn't mean that, and you know it,' Catherine's tone was brisk. 'I meant it makes you look vibrant—as though you've suddenly come alive. I wish you'd take Mary out on a shopping spree to find a few garments that'd give her a lift. Now then, Brett's pouring the drinks, so come along.'

As they walked along the passage towards the lounge Catherine's words echoed in Lisa's mind. *As though you've suddenly come alive.* Had Brett's kiss brought her to life? Certainly not, she told herself firmly. According to her own analysis it had been more in the form of an insult. Even so, her heart fluttered slightly as she entered the room.

He was standing at the cocktail cabinet, a glass of golden liquid in his hand, and she noticed he had changed into a well-cut jacket of dark brown which contrasted with his light tan trousers.

He turned and stared at her for several moments, his dark eyes raking her from head to foot before placing the glass on a small silver tray and carrying it to her. 'Very nice,' he murmured, his glance flicking to the cleavage at the deep neckline of her dress.

'Thank you.' She took a small sip. 'Yes, it *is* very nice. Is it a New Zealand sherry?'

'No, it's an Australian cream—one of Catherine's favourites, it's so smooth. But I wasn't referring to the sherry, as you were probably well aware.'

'No?' She looked up at him, innocent of the fact that her eyes shone and that an exuberance from within was reflected in her face.

Mary, still in her tan track-suit, spoke from the settee. 'Why did you bother to change?' she asked in a slightly petulant voice. 'Paul's not coming, you know.' The last words were spoken with a sharpness that betrayed an underlying suspicion.

Lisa ignored her tone. 'I hadn't forgotten. A prior engagement, wasn't it?'

'He said so, didn't he?' Mary snapped crossly, then went on ungraciously, 'Very well, if you've changed I suppose I'd better do likewise.' She put her glass down with a slight bang which caused the contents to splash, then left the room.

Catherine's eyes followed her exit before they turned to Brett. 'Is Mary annoyed about something?' she asked mildly.

He shrugged. 'It's possible she's disappointed because she expected Paul to be with us for dinner. I must admit I also expected him to be here—with bells on.' He turned to Lisa. 'Didn't you think he'd be with us for evening meal?'

She knew he watched her narrowly, but she sent him a look that was both wide-eyed and direct. 'I hadn't thought about it at all—however, I recall that one never could tell with Paul. He arrived if it suited him, otherwise he'd cook up a prior engagement.'

'Let's not talk about Paul,' Catherine said impatiently. She turned to Brett. 'Have you plans for tomorrow?'

'Yes. I've decided to examine the mountain track at the end of Lynton Road. I'm wondering if some of it has fallen away after the heavy rains we had earlier this month. I'm taking Lisa with me.'

Lisa was startled. 'You're taking me? Where, exactly?'

But before he could answer Catherine said. 'Oh, that'll be nice.' She turned to Lisa, a pleased expression on her face. 'Now you'll understand why I advised you to bring strong rubber boots with you. You did so, I hope?'

'Yes, I brought them—but it's the first I've heard of this particular outing.' She looked at Brett, awaiting further explanation, but he merely poured himself another sherry. She went on, 'Actually, I'd intended to continue with my reading project tomorrow. There's so much of it to get through.'

'How far have you got with it?' Catherine asked eagerly.

'I'm about to begin on the first six sailing vessels to reach this part of the colony.'

'You can forget them.' Brett snapped the words as an order. 'We'll set off before lunch with a pack of sandwiches, and we'll ride on my Honda farm bike—at least as far as it'll take us. Have you ever ridden on the back of a motorbike?'

She shook her head. 'No, nor am I sure that I want to!'

'Then you can look on it as a new experience. Have you ever walked in natural bush?' Again she shook her head. 'That'll be another new experience,' he pointed out drily.

Catherine protested, 'You're being very high-handed, Brett! She doesn't have to go with you if she doesn't want to. If she'd prefer to read about the early ships she's at liberty to do so.' She turned to Lisa. 'Some of them had ghastly voyages——'

Brett cut in, 'Leave it, Catherine. She'll read about them eventually, but not tomorrow, because she's coming with me. The bush is alive with birds and today's growth of native plants, which are much more interesting than yesterday's records of old sailing vessels.'

'We all have our own interests,' Catherine pointed out crossly. 'Mine is history. Yours is the mountain with its tracks, routes, vegetation and birdlife——'

'To say nothing of its geology,' he added as he refilled her glass.

Lisa remained silent as she wondered about the next day's outing. Why was it necessary for Brett to take her with him? Was it possible that he genuinely wished for her company? Her heart lifted at the thought and she knew it would be pleasant to share his interests for a few hours.

His voice broke into her musings. 'You're very quiet.'

She raised her eyes to his, knowing she must say something. 'I—I was just wondering if Mary has a special interest,' she prevaricated.

'Only her trousseau.' Brett's tone was sardonic.

'Most girls collect items for a bottom drawer or hope chest,' Catherine defended.

'Hope being the operative word,' added Brett.

Looking from one to the other, Lisa guessed the answer to her own question. Mary's special interest was Paul Mason, but whether she was *his* special interest was something yet to be learnt.

At that moment Mary returned to the room. She had changed into a jersey and skirt of drab brown which did little for her as it needed the addition of a bright-coloured scarf to give it a lift. And as she crossed self-consciously to the settee Lisa caught a resigned glance pass from Brett to Catherine, although neither made any comment.

'Drink up, you're behind us,' Brett said kindly.

Mary gulped the remains of her sherry and he refilled her glass.

Watching them, Lisa realised that Brett was fond of his sister. He wanted her to be happy, and in that moment she had a clearer understanding of his suspicions towards herself. However, only time would really assure him that she had not come to this place in search of Paul Mason.

During dinner Mary had little to say, and her silence made Lisa wonder if she also had begun building antagonism towards herself. Mary, she decided, needed diversion in the way of a change of environment, and Lisa could think of no better place than her own home on Auckland's North Shore.

Almost as though reading her thoughts Brett said, 'Tell us about life at home, Lisa. Is it very gay?'

She smiled. 'It depends upon what you call gay. At Takapuna, which is across the harbour bridge, we have the beach at our back door. We can swim in the sea, walk on the beach or sit beneath old pohutukawa trees that are covered with red blossoms at Christmas time. Most of my friends live on the North Shore, so it's never far from entertainment of some sort.'

'Your father's interests are on the North Shore?' Brett put the question politely.

'Yes. He's a barrister. During the summer evenings and at weekends he relaxes by going out on the harbour to fish from his launch.'

Catherine was interested. 'Your mother fishes as well?'

'No. She plays bridge, because she says it keeps her mind alert.' Lisa turned impulsively to Mary. 'When I leave here would you like to come home with me? You might enjoy a change at Takapuna.'

Mary shook her head, her eyes holding a sad expression. 'It's kind of you to suggest it, but no, thank you. I—I don't want to leave home at present.'

Brett became impatient. 'Snap out of it, Mary— you're wearing your doleful spaniel puppy look! What's the matter with you? Things are sure to be better tomorrow—just you wait and see!'

She gave him a wan smile before her face suddenly brightened. 'Do you think so?' she asked eagerly. 'Do you think that perhaps—I mean, have you any reason to believe——?'

'Of course. I'll bet on it,' he assured her.

Lisa was puzzled, trying to follow the trend of their rather vague conversation. Did Brett mean that things would improve tomorrow because Paul would be sure to arrive? And was this his reason for taking her to examine the mountain track? Was it his intention to get her out of the house so that Mary and Paul could have time alone together?

Her spirits plummeted. So much for his desire for her company! She must have been crazy to have imagined such a thought existing in his mind.

As though deliberately changing the subject Brett turned to Catherine. 'Gwen has excelled herself with this lot.' He poured more cream on the crusty apple and date dessert before him.

'Who's Gwen?' Lisa felt compelled to ask.

'Mrs Yates,' explained Catherine. 'She's the wife of Brett's farm manager, John Yates. She comes every day except Tuesday and at the weekend to do part-time work in this house. When I became so involved with my book I felt it was unfair to leave all the cooking and housework to Mary, so Gwen was only too pleased to earn some money.'

Brett said, 'Their house is the next one along Lynton Road. You'll see it as we pass.'

Mary sent him a sharp glance. 'Where are you going tomorrow?'

'To examine the Lynton track for wash-outs. Lisa will ride behind me on the bike.'

Mary giggled as she continued to brighten visibly. She smiled at Lisa and said, 'You'll have to sit mighty close to him and hang on tight with your arms round his waist.'

'Yes, I suppose so.' Unable to meet Brett's eyes, Lisa stared at her plate. The thought of clinging to him caused a tiny pulse to hammer in her throat and she could only hope her entire neck wasn't slowly becoming scarlet. She felt she had to say something, so she asked, 'Where does the name Lynton come from?'

'It was given by the first owner of this property, who came from Lynton in North Devon,' Brett told her. 'He applied for the right to mill the timber on this land, and years later the place became his son's estate. It was then put up for auction and purchased by my father.'

'It's hard to imagine those green fields as standing bush.'

'You'll see standing bush tomorrow,' he promised.

Next day it was after mid-morning when he ran critical eyes over Lisa's blue track-suit, jacket and rubber boots. 'You'll do,' he approved at last, then carefully placed a yellow motorcycle helmet on her head. 'See that you keep your arms firmly round my waist.'

She nodded as she watched him put a similar helmet on his own head. Nor did she need any second bidding as they made their way towards the blind end of Lynton Road, which dipped occasionally to cross small streams, then rose to wind between boxthorn hedges. It was an ever-upward grade, becoming steeper as they drew nearer the mountain, and at one high lookout point Brett stopped the Honda to give Lisa a panoramic view of the landscape below.

She gazed down on what appeared to be an enormous patchwork quilt of varied greens patterned with hedgerows and dotted with plantations of darker pines and macrocarpas; and despite its low undulations the land looked surprisingly flat, while peeps of the road they had recently traversed could be seen as a narrow strip of grey ribbon.

'The fields appear to be divided into rectangles,' she remarked.

'That's for rotational grazing,' Brett explained. 'The cows go into the fields first and clean up the long grass. They like to get their tongues round it and tear it off. Then the sheep are put in to nibble the shorter grass left closer to the ground. After that the field is given a rest to allow the sweet new grass to grow long again for the cows.'

He was standing close to her, his hand resting on her shoulder while he pointed out various landmarks, and as her gaze moved from north to south she became vitally conscious of his nearness. In fact it became an effort to keep her gaze directed towards the view instead of giving way to the urge to turn and look up into his face. She shook herself mentally. What on earth was the matter with her?

At last he turned towards the Honda, and as she clambered on to the seat behind him he adjusted the small canvas shoulder bag which hung at his side. It contained a thermos of coffee, mugs and two packs of sandwiches which Catherine had prepared for them. 'Hold on,' he commanded.

Lisa put her arms about his waist, then found difficulty in resisting the temptation to rest her head against his back. And again she told herself she was being idiotic. Nor did her chaotic thoughts allow her to notice how far they had ridden until they came to an area where the land had become littered with half-burnt stumps and fallen logs. The pale grey trunks of dead trees gave an air of desolation as their ghostly bare branches became silhouetted against the darkness of the nearby bush.

The road had now deteriorated into what was little more than a rough farm track, and a short distance further on Brett stopped the motorcycle near a stile set in the fence. They dismounted, removed their helmets which they left beside the bike, then moved towards the steps.

Brett said, 'You're about to enter the Egmont National Park by one of its back doors.' He sprang across the stile, then turned to offer Lisa assistance.

Avoiding the helping hand he held towards her, she said coolly, 'It's all right, I can manage, thank you.' But as she flung her leg across the top bar and began to descend her rubber boot slipped on the damp moss covering the step. She lunged forward and would have fallen if his arms had not caught and held her against him.

A gasp escaped her, and, aware that her heart was thudding, she laughed shakily as she looked up at him. 'That was stupid of me!'

But there was no laughter in the eyes that looked down at her. His mouth tightened and an intangible expression crossed his face. 'Let that be lesson number one,' he said grimly. 'I offered to assist you across, but you refused. In future you'll do as I say, particularly when we're in the bush. Agreed?'

'Yes, I'll remember.'

'Good.' He continued to hold her against him, his eyes still raking every feature of her face. Her heart quickened its pounding as she waited for his lips to descend towards her own, but this did not happen. Instead he released her abruptly, and she became conscious of an acute disappointment.

'Let's get going,' he snapped.

They left the sunshine and passed into the coolness of the bush, walking along the path where soggy dead leaves formed a damp brown carpet on the rich black soil. It was like stepping into an enchanted world where great tree trunks towered like stately grey pillars above the tangle of undergrowth.

At the same time she became conscious of an eeriness about the place. The stillness made her want to walk on tiptoe, while the silence forced her to whisper, 'It's like a fairy-tale forest!'

Her tension conveyed itself to him. 'Are you feeling nervous?'

She peered through the trees towards shadowed gloom that was pierced by shafts of golden sunlight, then admitted, 'Yes, perhaps I am a little.'

'Don't worry, there's no reason to be afraid. There are no snakes in New Zealand, even if some of those twisting mossy boughs look like green pythons. Would it help if you hold my hand?'

Lisa looked at him doubtfully. 'I know you're laughing at me. You probably think I'm an idiot.'

'Not at all,' he assured her gravely. 'The bush has an atmosphere that's entirely its own. It has the power to affect people until they become accustomed to it.'

She stood still, her eyes raised to the lofty limbs that met and entwined above their heads. 'It's like being in a cathedral.'

'Yes.' He held out his hand.

She grasped it gratefully, the firmness of his grip filling her with a feeling of security that swept away her previous intangible fears. And as she became aware of his quiet strength she also knew that here was a man who, once his word had been given, would prove to be steadfast.

A more peaceful frame of mind descended upon her as they walked along the path which continued to wind upward and became narrow as it rose towards the higher levels. In several places it fell away on one side, and these dangerous areas were recorded by Brett, who jotted their positions in a notebook.

There were also times when it was so steep and slippery it became necessary for him to literally drag her up the difficult slopes, and after one hazardous stretch she became so winded she leaned against a nearby tree to regain her breath.

'Is it too much for you?' he asked quietly, yet amused.

'Of course not,' she gasped crossly. 'It's just that— that I'm not used to it——'

'Are your legs aching?' There was the hint of a laugh in his voice.

'Not at all,' she lied, annoyed to be displaying the fact that she was unfit, while he himself gave hardly a puff of breathlessness. 'I'm sorry if I'm delaying you.'

He smiled. 'Don't let it concern you. I can see you're struggling gamely.' He dragged a long trailing strand of soft green moss from a low branch, then twisted it into a wreath which he placed on her head. 'For such valiant effort you'll be crowned princess of the bush.'

Her gay laugh rang on the stillness. 'Oh, thank you—I'll have to do something about finding a prince——' She stopped, appalled by her own words, then found herself unable to meet his eyes.

'You haven't found him yet?' he asked slyly.

'*No!*' The denial came abruptly because she suspected he had Paul in mind. The thought made her want to snatch the wreath from her head, but to do so would ruin the fragile friendship that was stretching between them like a tender vine.

Brett regarded her anxiously. 'Would you prefer to go back? I can come alone another day.'

She shook her head, knowing she longed to be with him.

As they continued along the ever-ascending path he told her a little about the numerous tracks and routes on the mountain, then explained, 'A route is one that's newly-cut and is not to be travelled alone by inexperienced people.'

'You mean by people like me,' she said ruefully. 'People who slip and slide and who can't keep their footing while climbing over an ordinary stile?'

'It's all right so long as they have someone nearby to catch them,' he added pointedly.

Lisa caught her breath, realising that he recalled how closely he had held her—and then his next words brought further irritation.

'I suppose Paul took you up to the North Egmont Chalet or to the Stratford Mountain House?'

Frustrated, she almost stamped her foot. 'No, he did *not!*'

'Okay, there's no need to get mad. One day we'll take a trip up to the Dawson Falls Tourist Lodge. It'll take you higher than we are now, which is about two thousand feet.' He fell silent as he stared up into the branches. 'Look, a native pigeon and its mate. They'll be searching for berries.'

Her eyes followed his pointing finger to where the two plump birds sat, a shaft of sunlight catching their multi-coloured metallic backs and wings, their snowy-white breasts and abdomens. 'Do you see them?' Brett whispered in her ear, his hand on her shoulder, his lips almost brushing her cheek.

'They're beautiful,' she breathed, doing her utmost to remain calm and to ignore his disturbing nearness. But even as she spoke there was a sudden whoosh of wings and the birds disappeared into the higher branches of the trees.

They continued to push upward until they reached a point where the path ended by being crossed by a wider and more substantial track. Brett guided her towards the left, and within a short time they came to a bench seat. She sank on to it thankfully, then watched while he took the thermos and two packs of sandwiches from the canvas shoulder-bag.

Behind them a hill covered with shining mountain flax rose so steeply it formed an almost perpendicular wall, while before them the ground sloped down to a mossy hollow which had the large trunk of a tree lying across its shallow basin.

The sight of it sent a feeling of sadness through Lisa. 'It's a fallen giant,' she said. 'It took so many years to grow, yet it fell so quickly. The surrounding undergrowth and overhead foliage appear to be sheltering it.'

Brett said, 'Forget the tree and drink this.' He handed her a mug of steaming coffee.

She sipped it gratefully. 'Thank you. I don't know when I've walked uphill for such a long distance. My legs are feeling weak and shaky.' She hadn't meant to admit this last fact.

'You'll find it easier going downhill. People who live near the mountain become used to it,' he added casually.

She laughed. 'What makes you imagine I'll be here long enough to do that?'

He remained silent, staring moodily ahead of him.

Lisa relaxed, savouring the inexplicable pleasure of sitting beside him, then, biting into a sandwich made of cold meat and tomato relish, she remarked, 'This relish is very tasty.'

'Yes, it's one of Catherine's specialities. She's very capable and she's been a damned good stepmother to us, even to the extent of doing her best to get Mary off the shelf.'

'I presume you mean with Paul?'

'Yes. She's a real manipulator. She met him at his uncle's funeral, and it didn't take long for her to recognise that here was an eligible bachelor who'd be living next door. She invited him in for meals, no doubt hoping to line him up with Mary.'

'Do you mean she was deliberately—*matchmaking*?' queried Lisa.

'A more blatant example of matchmaking I've yet to see.'

Lisa rose to Catherine's defence. 'I can understand her wishing to see Mary happily married.' There was a momentary silence until a mischievous imp forced her to add, 'And I would also expect her to have your happiness at heart. No doubt she considers it high time you were settled down and married.'

Brett shrugged, then his voice became hard. 'It's possible—but if so she can forget it. She may consider herself to be President of the Manipulating Society, but she needn't imagine she can put her tactics to work where I'm concerned.'

Lisa turned to look at him. 'She's—she's already tried?'

Brett's mouth became grim. 'Not yet, but I can assure you that any girl brought into my house with a view to matrimony will get short shrift. She'll be tossed out on her neck—and right smartly at that!'

# CHAPTER FOUR

THE icy tone of Brett's words cut into her mind like a blast from the Arctic. And as she watched the handsome profile from the corner of her eye she saw that his dark brows were drawn into a scowl while his mouth remained twisted in a grim line.

Did Catherine really believe he could be manipulated into marriage? she wondered. The idea was ludicrous, because here was a man with a mind of his own. Once it was made up it would remain that way until he changed it of his own accord.

In this respect he was completely unlike Paul, who found much difficulty in settling down to one project or person for any length of time. He reminded Lisa of a buck rabbit that ran all over the field, first with one doe and then another, and she was thankful she had learnt this fact in time.

Choosing her words carefully, she said, 'It's obvious that Mary likes Paul very much, but is she really in love with him?'

'It's impossible to say. Whatever the case you'll recall that I've indicated that I don't want to see her hurt. Would it upset you if Paul and Mary became engaged?' The abrupt question matched the coolness of the glance he swept over her.

She ignored the continued iciness in his manner as she forced herself to give a light laugh. 'It *would* concern me, but not for the reason you imagine.'

'Perhaps you could be a little more explicit,' he invited.

'Definitely not. It's something you'll just have to find out for yourself, as no doubt you will when the time comes. Do you mind if we change the subject? It's beginning to bore me.'

'Okay. What would you prefer to talk about?'

She raked in her mind for a suitable topic, then decided to talk in terms of his own interests. 'Tell me about your Search and Rescue work. I've heard so little about it.'

'Are you sure you'd be interested?' he demanded dryly.

'Would I ask if I were not?'

He appeared to be slightly gratified, because the coldness left his voice as he said, 'You probably know that in New Zealand the Search and Rescue Organisation operates to save life. It's mainly concerned with missing aircraft or ships in distress, while our section of it is involved with people who are injured or lost in the mountains or bush country.'

'Have there been many deaths on Mount Egmont?' she asked.

'Far too many. It's a deceptive mountain because it looks so easy. People can reach the base of it without any trouble, and many who are ill-equipped and lack experience are tempted to try an ascent. They become involved in difficulties within an hour or so of leaving their cars.'

'What sort of difficulties?' Lisa felt compelled to ask.

'Oh, they tumble over precipices, get lost on side tracks, or fall into holes where the earth has been washed away by springs. There are also swamps to be avoided.' Warming to his subject, he went on to tell her about the dangers of climbing alone, and to list the rules learnt by all who go tramping on the mountain. Then he ended by saying, 'Most of the accidents on Egmont have been caused by idiots who disregarded these rules.' He glanced at his watch. 'Well, if your legs are okay, it's time we were getting back.'

'Of course they're okay. Do you think I'm a poor weak fool?' she asked indignantly as she began packing the thermos and mugs into the bag.

'It remains to be seen.' He sent her one of his rare smiles, then stood up and crossed the path to stare more intently at the fallen tree lying across the hollow below them. 'Shades of Chew Chong!' he exclaimed. 'Some of his precious Jew's ear is growing on the trunk of that dead tree!'

'Oh——?' Lisa moved to stand beside him and peer downwards.

'Do you see that brown curly fungus growing in rows along the lower curve on the trunk? That's the famous "Taranaki wool" gathered by the settlers of earlier days.'

Staring down at the trunk, she exclaimed eagerly, 'I'd like to take a closer look at it.'

Brett chuckled. 'You intend to slide down on your seat? It's much steeper than you realise.'

'I can see it's steep—and I shall not slide,' she told him loftily as she looked from left to right, examining access to the fallen tree. 'See, there's an easier grade farther along. I'm sure I can reach it without any trouble.'

He looked down at her rubber boots. 'I don't advise it,' he drawled. 'Trouble could lurk down there.'

'I *must* have a closer look at that Jew's ear,' she persisted. 'What's more, I intend to gather some.'

'Don't say you haven't been warned,' he remarked casually. 'Jew's ear grows best in swampy areas.'

'That ground looks quite firm to me,' she said with a quiet determination. At least she'd show him she wasn't going to be bossed. *At least*—not all the time.

She left his side and walked along the track to where it dropped until it was almost level with the fallen trunk. Then she pushed her way back through the thick scrubby mass of undergrowth until she came out into the clearer area near the tree. She knew that he stood watching her progress from the track above, and she also knew he was grinning broadly.

'Is my wish to examine the fungus so very funny?' she demanded.

'Not at all. Keep going.' There was the suspicion of a laugh behind his words, almost as though he expected something to happen.

It did within the next few moments. Lisa moved forward again, but had taken only a few steps when she stopped with a small gasp as her feet began to sink. There was a wet slosh as she lifted first one foot and then the other, hastily attempting to step backward and almost losing her balance.

'Let me know when it's over your knees,' Brett called mockingly.

She sent him an angry accusing glare. 'You *knew* there was a swamp here—you *knew* it'd be like this!'

'I didn't—but I guessed. I told you Jew's ear grows in swampy patches, and I advised you against going near the place,' he reminded her smugly. 'Some people won't take advice—they just have to learn the hard way.'

She took a few more steps, then shrieked in terror. 'I can't find the firm ground that got me here—I keep sinking—*help!*'

She looked up pleadingly, but to her horror he had disappeared. Panic gripped her as she wondered if he was so annoyed he had left her to struggle out of her own predicament. How could he? she thought hysterically—*how could he?*

'Brett!' she yelled, her fear-filled voice echoing on the still air. '*Brett, come back!*'

'I'm coming.' His voice spoke from behind as he began to push his way through the undergrowth. 'I'll make sure of firm footing.'

She knew he leaned forward and that his arms dragged her from the dangerous area that slowly sucked at her boots. She felt herself being lifted and carried from the spot, then she was set down in the midst of the leafy undergrowth. But instead of his arms leaving her body they held her against his muscular length.

His voice came from above her head. 'Well, are you satisfied?'

She nodded without speaking as she leaned against him, overwhelmed by relief yet feeling idiotic.

'And you really thought I'd leave you?' The words lashed at her.

'I—I really didn't know. I can understand that you're mad with me, and I suppose you think I'm completely stupid——' Shivers ran through her body as several other suppositions swept into her mind. Suppose she'd come to this place alone? Suppose Brett hadn't been near to lift her out of that ghastly place where she might have sunk further and further into the swamp?

The thought made her cling to him with a compulsive movement, but suddenly she became aware that his hands had moved to her shoulders and that he was staring down into her face.

Shaking her, he gritted furiously, 'Now do you understand how dangerous it can be when inexperienced fools break the rules? *Never* leave the main track to explore alone!'

She stared up at him dumbly, while an unexpected rush of tears filled her eyes, but before she could brush them away his arms were again holding her close to him. He lowered his head and kissed her fiercely, almost as though to punish her and to give vent to his own anger.

The spasm of rage passed as quickly as it had begun. He looked at her without speaking for several moments, then, slowly and gently, he again lowered his head. His mouth drew near to her own, and as their lips met her arms crept about his neck.

Emotions within her were shocked to wakefulness, spinning her blood into whirlpools as his hard mouth became more and more possessive. Her lips parted as she responded with a sudden wild ecstasy that was beyond her power to control.

As his kiss deepened she felt his hands find their way beneath her jacket to encircle her waist, then briefly cup her breasts before moving to slide down her spine. She knew they had spread themselves over her hips, and as they crushed her against him with sensual intimacy she became aware of the naked desire coursing through her veins.

At last his lips left her mouth to trail along her jaw and nuzzle a throbbing pulse in her neck; then, returning to her lips again, his kiss became devouring, while she gave herself up to the rapture of its bliss.

A deep sigh seemed to shake him as he murmured huskily, 'Lisa, you don't know what you do to me— can you hear me calling?'

She nodded, feeling too emotionally full to speak.

'I could make the world stand still for you,' he whispered.

She nodded again, knowing that during the last few moments of those searing kisses the world had indeed stood still.

'A swamp is not the best place for making love.' His voice was low and intense.

Lisa gave a small shaky laugh, having difficulty in finding an answer to this blunt statement. 'I'm afraid I—I know little or nothing about making love,' she admitted shyly as she hid her face against his neck.

'Didn't Paul teach you to make love?' he demanded, the iron in his voice making it sound harsh.

She was startled. 'Paul? *Never!* If you must know the truth, I've never made love with any man.'

'From the response in your kisses, that's hard to believe.'

His words shocked her, dampening her ardour more effectively than a blast of sleet in her face, and she began to recall the last time he had kissed her. On that occasion she had wondered if his passionate embrace had been sincere, or had he intended it to be a means of diverting her interest away from Paul. So was this also merely an act on Mary's behalf?

The suspicion made her feel ill, causing her to quiver slightly as she pushed against his chest to avoid further close contact.

Brett released her at once. 'You're trembling,' he accused. 'Is it rage, or are you afraid of me?'

She looked up into the penetrating dark eyes, then shook her head. 'No, it is not rage, nor is it fear of you that bothers me. Perhaps distrust would be a better word.'

'Distrust?' The black brows drew together. '*You*— distrust *me*? Well, I'll be damned! Would you mind explaining that remark?' His voice betrayed both surprise and anger.

Lisa leaned against him in silence, unable to utter the words that would expose her thoughts; nor did she wish to go into the details of her suspicions concerning his reasons for kissing her with such intensity. To do so would be to openly accuse him of blatant insincerity.

A short silence followed while she pondered the extent of his anger, and even as she did so he gripped her arms, his fingers biting with strength through her jacket. 'I could give you a damned good shaking, Lisa Longmore,' he gritted. 'I demand that you explain yourself!'

The words clicked her mind into action, forcing her to step back and glare up at him. 'You *demand*? I'm not in the habit of bowing to the demands of any man. Nor have I anything further to say.'

'Very well——' He turned on his heel and threw a terse remark over his shoulder. 'Let's get going—it's high time we were on our way home.'

Despite her own burning resentment Lisa followed obediently, conscious that he was really angry and that her foolish tongue had caused a barrier to rise between them. They reached the track in silence, Brett flung the strap of the canvas bag across his shoulder, then strode along rapidly leaving her to hasten after him.

She found the return journey less arduous because it was downhill, nevertheless there were difficulties caused by slippery areas where, without his helping hand, she found herself sliding on mud only lightly covered by leaves. And although she did her best to keep up with him his long strides gradually took him ahead to lengthen the distance between them.

Nor did he trouble to glance back to assure himself she was not lagging too far in the rear, and, watching him disappear through the trees ahead, she felt hurt and depressed. It was obvious that he cared little about her, despite the ardour of his caresses to which she had been foolish enough to respond. *You idiot!* she chided herself mentally with inward raging.

Very well, Brett Arlington, she fumed silently, you can break into a gallop for all I care—and when you reach the edge of the bush you can cool your heels and wait for me. And with this thought firmly in her mind she lessened her pace and deliberately loitered by leaning against a tree to catch her breath.

But moments later she was on her way again, hurrying along the path and making sure she didn't veer from its main course. It would be easy to do this, she realised, because in some places there were side tracks, and it was while glancing along one of them that she tripped over a protruding root and was sent sprawling into a hollow beneath the curving fronds of low-growing tree-ferns. For several moments she lay winded and gasping for breath in a bed of leaf mould, and just as she was about to struggle to her feet she heard his voice calling her name.

'Lisa—Lisa! Cooee, *Lisa!*'

A devil prompted her to lie still and remain silent.

'Lisa, *Lisa*, where the hell are you——?'

His voice, vibrating with anxiety and frustration, was closer now, his footsteps nearer and heavy, and she knew he was hastening along the path to find her. However, she continued to remain still, smiling to herself as she realised his fear of her becoming lost along a side track had brought him pounding back in a frantic effort to find her.

Peeping through the fern fronds, she saw that he was well past her hiding place, so she scrambled out of the hollow and without waiting to brush the leaf mould from her jacket she sped along the track. When she reached the edge of the bush she climbed over the stile with care, then went to stand beside the motorbike and await his return.

At last she became aware that he was staring at her from the shadow of the bush on the other side of the stile. 'Hi there!' she called gaily, yet conscious of a guilty twinge. 'Where have you been? I wondered if you'd got lost.'

Brett vaulted the stile and strode towards her, his face grim. 'Where the devil did *you* get to?' he rasped, disregarding her bantering tone.

She sent him a faint smile. 'Oh, I climbed a couple of trees.'

'Like hell you did!' His eyes narrowed as they observed traces of leaf mould still clinging to her jacket. 'You've been lying on the ground. Did you have a fall?'

'A slight tumble into a hollow,' she admitted evasively, not daring to admit she could have stopped him from thundering past.

'Hell's bells, you gave me the devil of a fright! It's so easy to wander off the main track.' The next instant he had snatched her to him, kissing her with a savage force that was both hard and cruel enough to bruise her lips.

She knew he was giving vent to his anger, and steeled herself against response of any kind until he released her abruptly. Glaring at him furiously, she hissed, 'You kiss me like that once more and I'll pack my bags! I'll tell Catherine to find somebody else to edit her book. Or is that what you're really aiming at? You'd like me to leave, wouldn't you? Go on—admit it!'

His eyes glittered as he drew a deep breath and grabbed the handles of the bike. 'Get on,' he ordered coldly. 'And hang on tightly or you'll be flung off at a corner. Nor shall I bother to stop and pick you up.'

The next instant the motor roared, the bike slithered and skidded, then sped down the hill.

The return journey took only a short time, speed being the main factor. Lisa clung to Brett, her arms clasped tightly round his waist, and although he swerved around corners, swept up hills and down gullies to almost bounce over small bridges, they arrived home without mishap.

He stopped in the back yard, where she put her feet to the ground with the utmost relief. 'Thank you,' she said as she unfastened the motorcycle helmet. 'Do you always ride like a bat out of hell?' Then she went inside, leaving him to put the bike in the shed.

Catherine greeted her as she entered the kitchen. 'Ah, you're back. I was beginning to fear Brett might have taken you too far along those bush tracks. Once he gets going he never knows when to stop. Did you enjoy it up there?'

'Oh yes, I loved it,' Lisa admitted with enthusiasm, then was startled to realise she wasn't thinking of the trees or the bush tracks at all, but of the fact that Brett's arms had been about her, holding her close to him, his lips on her own. The memory sent a surge of quivering excitement through her, and, fearing that Catherine's sharp eyes might detect the flush that was making her cheeks feel hot, she said hastily, 'I think I'll have a shower and change out of this track-suit.'

'A good idea,' Catherine agreed. 'It'll take any stiffness out of you and help you to relax before the evening meal. We're just having Mary's special fish pie with mashed potatoes and green peas, and she's even made date scones to have with our coffee. She's in the lounge with Paul.'

Lisa stared at her, but said nothing, and as she went to her bedroom her heart sank at the thought of Paul joining them at the table. He would be sure to come up with embarrassing remarks of some sort, either to make Mary jealous or to deliberately needle herself. Her best plan would be to ignore him, she decided.

The hot shower streaming over her slim naked body had its soothing effect on her tired muscles, but did nothing to lessen the fears of what attitude Paul might take, or what tactics he might apply. To him it would all be very amusing, something to chuckle about for days to come. So *ignore him*, she reminded herself.

She recalled his old habit of dropping hints and adding innuendoes to embellish an event, and she knew he was more than capable of giving Brett the impression that their previous relationship had had its moments of sexual intimacy, when in fact such had not been the case.

Nor had this been through lack of pleading on Paul's part. He had done his best to get Lisa into bed, but for some inexplicable reason she had always drawn back before taking that final step from which there would be no return. Her continued refusal had infuriated Paul, who had declared she didn't love him, and this, she had eventually realised, had been the truth of the matter.

She dressed slowly to prolong the moment of meeting him, and at the same time she became aware of her own confused emotions. Vague depressions gripped her, but they were swept away by the memory of Brett's arms holding her close, and she knew she wanted to appear attractive in his eyes.

In an effort to do so she put on a pleated skirt and matching top of fine wool, the shade of deep cream contrasting with her dark auburn hair. Gold earrings and a gold chain pendant added just the right note, and as she surveyed herself in the long mirror on the wardrobe door she wondered if Brett would give her as much as a second glance.

Irritation from Paul began the moment she stepped into the lounge. He was sitting on the settee beside Mary, but he stood up as she entered, an affable grin spreading across his face. 'Lisa, my dear, how charming you look!' he exclaimed with more force than necessary. 'But then you always did have a flair for clothes.'

She sent him a brief glance but ignored the remark.

He went on, 'Isn't that the dress you wore on our last outing together?'

'Certainly not,' she snapped crossly. 'It's almost new.'

'But you had one like it—a sort of pale lemon colour?'

'No, I did not,' she retorted angrily. Then, ignoring her former decision to disregard his remarks, she changed her mind and impulsively decided to stand up to him. 'Please don't try to give the impression that you remember my clothes, Paul, because that's too ridiculous for words.'

A lazy insinuating smile seemed to emphasise his next words. 'You're quite mistaken, my dear. I do remember—*everything*.'

'In that case you can stop calling me your dear, because you'll also remember it's a title that does *not* apply to me.'

'Ah, but it did.'

'Never in the *sincere* sense of the word,' she lashed back, then stopped abruptly as she became aware that she was on the verge of screaming at him in open warfare, and this, when she was a guest in the Arlington household, would be unforgivable.

She also knew the other people in the room were listening to this exchange with avid interest. Mary's brown eyes were wide in a face that had gone suddenly pale, while Brett had taken on the attitude of a watchful fox. And although Catherine must have been aware of the tension between Lisa and Paul, she appeared to ignore it, and in fact began to make excuses for Lisa.

Speaking to Paul from the depths of her armchair, she said, 'Take no notice of Lisa if she sounds tired. Brett has been dragging her up and down the mountain. I'm sure she's really delighted to see you, just as you must be pleased to see her.'

'You can say that again!' The grin was back on Paul's face.

Brett came to stand beside Lisa, the silver tray in his hand bearing a glass of sherry. His deep voice was sardonic as he said, 'In fact he's so darned pleased to see you he's brought a couple of bottles of wine to celebrate the fact that you're here.'

'It's your old favourite,' Paul told her smugly.

She felt nettled. '*My favourite?* I never had a favourite!'

'Oh yes, you did,' Paul argued. 'It's that Spanish one we had during the weekend your parents spent in New Plymouth. Do you recall how very well your father and I got on?'

She shook her head, forcing herself to remain calm. 'No, I'm afraid I don't remember.' Brash was the only term she could recall her father applying to Paul; nor had he hestitated to criticise her choice of male friends.

Catherine appeared to sense the controlled irritation in Lisa's voice, and her desire to get away from the subject of Paul's reminiscences. She turned to Brett. 'I haven't asked you about your trip up the mountain. Was the Lynton track in good order?'

He nodded. 'So far there are only a few minor wash-outs to be reported,' he told her.

'There was nothing of special interest?' she queried archly, with a quick glance towards Lisa.

'Special interest?' He was thoughtful for a few moments before his perceptive dark eyes also turned to Lisa and appeared to scan the thoughts swirling about in her mind. 'Do you consider we found anything—special?'

She turned away, unable to meet his gaze and fearful of the telltale colour she felt creeping into her cheeks. 'You stopped to jot several memos in your notebook,' she managed to remind him calmly. 'I wouldn't know how important they were—in fact I wouldn't know how important *anything* was.'

'How far did you go?' Mary asked.

He described the position of the seat, then added, 'Lisa saw her first growth of Jew's ear fungus today, but she couldn't get quite near enough to gather it.' There was a wicked glint in his eyes.

Payul leaned forward. 'I'm sure I showed you Jew's ear.'

Lisa shook her head, then looked at him steadily. 'You probably pointed it out to one of the many girl-friends you had during those days.' She glanced at Mary, hoping she'd got the message.

Mary had, but her irritation rebounded towards Lisa herself. She sent a look of anger across the room, but controlled herself as she stood up abruptly and said, 'Our fish pie will be ready now. I'll take it from the oven.'

But when Lisa sat at the table she found her appetite had deserted her. Paul's eyes constantly strayed towards her and she was aware that Brett watched them both without appearing to do so. The knowledge caused an inner agitation that forced her to merely toy with her food, and she was filled with acute embarrassment when Mary spoke to her from across the table.

'You don't have to eat it if you don't like it,' she said with a touch of irritation.

Lisa pulled herself together. 'Oh, I like it—it's very

nice. It's just that sometimes I eat rather slowly.
Perhaps I could have the recipe for it?' Mentally she
told herself to snap out of it. She was being a fool to
allow the situation to get under hr skin. And why was
she in this state of nervous upset? She frowned,
staring at her plate as she realised it was because of
Brett. But why should *he* affect her in this manner? It
was something she was unable to understand.

Nor were matters improved when Paul leaned
forward and spoke to her in earnest tones. 'I've
noticed several Auckland firms advertising for quali-
fied accountants. I'm toying with the idea of
applying to one of them—especially if it's on the
North Shore.'

Lisa's heart sank at his words. She was afraid to
look at either Brett or Mary, but before she could
think of anything to say Catherine's voice came
sharply.

'Are you saying you'd leave your farm?' she
demanded as she eyed Paul with surprise and sudden
disapproval.

He grinned at her. 'A change is as good as a rest. I'd
put my share-milker in full control while I gave myself
two or three years enjoying the city lights.'

'Two or three years!' Mary echoed faintly. She had
gone pale, and her brown eyes, now wide and full of
accusation, turned to Lisa as though blaming her for
Paul's decision.

'You mean you'd be away for only a period?'
Catherine persisted as though trying to pin him down
to something definite.

'Of course.' The grin flashed over his face. 'One
always comes home to the mountain—at least,
eventually.'

'It's part of that old mountain magic,' added Brett,
obviously making an attempt to console the depression
he knew to be simmering in Mary's mind.

'Magic, *rubbish!*' Mary snapped.

'Well, perhaps not actually magic,' he conceded, 'but everyone knows the upper slopes are supposed to be *tapu*—or taboo—to the Maori people. They won't go near them because some of the ancient chiefs were buried there and it's said their spirits refuse to leave the place.'

'What's holding them back?' asked Lisa, thankful for the change of subject.

Brett said, 'Years ago I tried to probe the answer from an elderly Maori woman, but she was vague.' His voice changed to a soft Maori dialect as he repeated her words. 'You know, it that old Taranaki fellow himself. He the magic mountain. The spirits of them chiefs, they just don't want to leave. In the old days, before you white people come to take our land, that mountain, he belong to them. When they die their spirits set off to go back to Hawaiki where the Maori people come from. But do they go? No. That old mountain, he call them back, and there they are to this day——'

Mary cut in scathingly, 'Where they waft about in the mist on rainy days.' Her chin rose as she glared at Brett. 'I know all this is an attempt to convince me that Paul will be back, but I know better. As soon as he gets to Auckland he'll put down roots and he'll stay there.' She turned to Paul. 'Isn't that true?'

'What makes you so sure about it?' Paul protested evasively.

Mary's voice rose slightly. 'Because *Lisa* will be there, that's why! She came here to find you, she's been successful, and now she'll take you home with her!'

'Control yourself, Mary,' Brett snapped angrily. 'You're behaving like a silly half-witted schoolgirl!'

Paul remained silent but had the grace to look embarrassed, while Catherine and Brett looked at Lisa, waiting for her to say something.

She found difficulty in searching for words, but at

last she turned to Paul and looked at him thoughtfully. She didn't want to be rude or hurtful, but her concern was for Mary—and if Mary hadn't latched on to the previous message here was the opportunity to send her another. So she said in quiet but serious tones, 'I don't think Mary realises that your temperament requires constant change, Paul.'

Paul's manner grew sulky. 'I don't know what you're talking about.'

'I think you do,' Lisa pursued calmly. 'Where girls were concerned your watchword was safety in numbers—at least it was when I knew you in New Plymouth.'

Mary sprang to Paul's defence. 'I don't believe a word you're saying!' she flared at Lisa. 'You're just being nasty to Paul. You're jealous because you know he's my—my friend!'

Lisa's eyes were full of sympathy as they rested on Mary, then she turned to Paul. Choosing her words carefully, she said, 'Really, Paul, in all fairness to Mary you should explain that change is the name of the game.'

Catherine's eyes flashed as she turned her attention to Paul. 'Is this a fact?' she asked quietly. 'Is this what you meant when you said a change is as good as a rest?'

He lifted his shoulders in a faint shrug, then smiled at her disarmingly. 'You're too intelligent not to realise that the mind is made to be changed, otherwise it becomes static.'

'I see.' She looked at him as though seeing him clearly for the first time. 'But surely you don't place *fidelity* within this reasoning?'

'Of course not,' he denied swiftly. 'At least, not if a definite commitment has been made.'

Lisa said nothing as she looked at him steadily, but he failed to meet her eyes. Nevertheless she felt a certain amount of satisfaction in having brought to light this particular trait in Paul's character, and perhaps it would give Mary something to dwell on—if only she'd be sensible enough to think about it.

At the same time she felt a tiny twinge of guilt, fearing that she might have been somewhat harsh on Paul, but this feeling vanished when the image of Maggie Simpson and her small son with the fair hair and light blue eyes flashed across her memory.

Later, when the plates had been stacked into the dishwasher, she was overcome by weariness, and, asking to be excused, she said to Catherine, 'I'm afraid I've wasted too much time during the weekend. I'll take the manuscript to bed and spend some time reading.'

Brett followed her into the library, his face set. 'I heard what you said to Catherine,' he gritted. 'So coming out with me was a waste of time? Thank you very much. *Bored*, were you?'

She lifted a chapter of *Mountain Memory* from the table, then turned to face him. 'I didn't mean it the way you imagine,' she informed him coolly, 'but you must realise that the sooner I get this job done, the sooner I'll be on my way back to Auckland.'

'With Paul following hard on your heels!' he snarled at her.

She ignored the remark and brushed past him, clutching the typewritten pages to her chest. But when she was in bed it became impossible to concentrate on the troubles, trials and earthquakes that shook the early settlements of Taranaki. Instead she saw only the dark images of Brett Arlington.

At last she laid the manuscript aside and stared unseeingly across the room. Had she met her own personal earthquake in the form of this man? The mere thought of him was beginning to shake her sufficiently to send the blood pounding through her veins.

But she was being a fool, she told herself firmly.

Brett had no real feeling for her, and if she allowed him to get a grip on her heart she would be completely insane. And with this decision she snatched up the manuscript and made a further determined effort to read, frowning at the pages as she scanned the lines.

Nevertheless, before she fell asleep she slipped out of bed and crossed the room to stand at the window. Gazing beyond the near fields towards the shadowy rising bush-clad slopes, and at the moonlight glistening on the high snowy peak, she spoke softly.

'Huh, you and your magic, Taranaki! You can call and call, but I'll not hear you. I'll return to Auckland—*and there I'll remain!*'

# CHAPTER FIVE

THE next morning was wet. Rain poured from a leaden sky, drenching the gardens and forming ponds in various parts of the lawn. The mountain, wrapped in a mantle of low thick cloud, was entirely invisible.

When Lisa went into the kitchen for breakfast there was no sign of either Brett or Mary. Brett's absence disappointed her, yet not for the world would she ask his whereabouts. However, the information inadvertently came from Catherine.

'Did the phone wake you early this morning?' she asked. 'John Yates rang for Brett to come as quickly as possible. It appears that two of the pedigree cows had decided to calve at the same time and both seemed to be having difficulties. These things always happen on a dirty wet day. The vet's with them now and all's well, especially as they've both given birth to heifer calves.'

'And Mary—where is she?' Lisa was almost afraid to ask the question, fearing that perhaps the previous evening's irritations were preventing Mary from joining them at the breakfast table.

But Catherine's explanation reassured her. 'She's gone to Stratford to see if she can match wool for a jersey she's knitting. She said she'll be away for most of the day, so you'll be able to work undisturbed. Brett lit the fire in the library before he left, so the room should be nice and warm.'

And indeed it was. Lisa looked at the blazing pine logs and at the well-filled woodbox, realising that despite the worry of the cows Brett had still found time to attend to her comfort. It was typical of him,

she thought, recognising that he was a man of few
words but plenty of action.

The dullness of the morning caused her to switch on
the standard lamp, then, drawing its glow nearer the
fire, she curled up in an armchair with another chapter
of Catherine's manuscript. As Gordon Bishop had
said, the book was far too long, but apart from that
fault Lisa was pleasantly surprised by its construction
and by Catherine's style of writing.

When Catherine brought coffee in at mid-morning
Lisa stretched herself, then sipped the hot drink
gratefully. 'Have you heard how the new calves are
progressing?' she asked.

It was really another way of asking if Brett had
returned, but apparently he had not, because
Catherine said, 'No, but they'll be in the vet's good
hands.' She chatted for a few more minutes, then
gathered the mugs and said, 'Well, I'll leave you to get
on with it.'

Lisa continued to read, skimming through the pages
rapidly as this was only the preliminary part of the
long task ahead. When lunchtime came she went to the
dining room fully expecting Brett to be in for the
midday meal, but still there was no sign of him. The
room seemed empty without his dominant presence,
and it was difficult to disguise her disappointment,
which was more acute than she cared to admit.

Catherine kept up a flow of chatter as she served a
rich vegetable soup, some of it about Mary, but most
of it about Brett. It was easy to see that she was very
fond of them both, and it was almost as though she
was taking advantage of their absence to inform Lisa
of their domestic situation.

'They've been good stepchildren to me,' she said
reminiscently. 'When their father died the property
was left equally among the three of us. However, a
legacy from their mother's parents had been well
invested for them, and it wasn't long before Brett was

in a position to buy not only my share of the place, but Mary's as well. It means he's the owner of Lynton, which is a valuable property.'

Lisa felt that a comment of some sort was expected of her. 'One would never doubt that he's the master of the establishment,' she remarked. 'He's really quite forceful——'

'And Brett's a most eligible man,' Catherine added, her hazel eyes holding a speculative gleam as they rested upon Lisa. 'Personally, I consider it high time he found himself a wife.'

For some reason Lisa found difficulty in meeting her eyes. 'I'm sure he'll do that, when it suits him.' Then, hesitantly, 'When that time comes, you'll continue to live here?'

'Oh no. When Brett marries I'll buy a flat in New Plymouth and Mary will probably live with me—unless she herself is already married by then.'

Lisa felt she had to ask the question. 'You'd like to see her married to Paul Mason?'

Catherine frowned. 'I thought so at one time, but now I'm not so sure. All that talk about *change* last night has made me wonder about it, but I suppose Mary's association with him will just have to run its course.'

'I'm sure it will,' agreed Lisa, then, not wishing to become involved in a discussion about Paul, she escaped back into the library, where she again buried her head in the manuscript.

It was late afternoon before she saw Brett. He strode into the room carrying more short lengths of bluegum for the woodbox, and as she looked at him she felt herself so strongly drawn towards him it wasn't funny. At last she dragged her eyes from the darkness of his hair which contrasted with the maize colour of his polo-necked jersey. 'How is the bovine maternity ward?' she asked.

'Mothers and daughters all doing well.' He came

closer to look at her critically. 'Have you been reading all day? Your eyes are beginning to look like a couple of burnt holes in a cream blanket!'

'Thank you for the kind words——' Her voice faltered as she saw his gaze move to rest on her lips, and as his thoughts seemed to reach out to her she became conscious of quickening pulses and the slight flush that began to steal into her cheeks.

At last she felt she had to say something. 'I'll admit I've kept at it fairly solidly. I can understand Catherine's mind becoming involved with the past. Small glimpses make one want to see more.'

'Those early years challenged the courage of everyone. I know I'd have enjoyed them.' Brett's hands gripped her shoulders as he turned her to face him. 'Would you have enjoyed being there too? What sort of a pioneer wife would you have made, Lisa Longmore?'

His action had been unexpected, and she looked at him, puzzled. Did he mean—*with him?* Not daring to presume such a thing, she said, 'Not a very good one, I'm afraid. I'd have been terrified, especially during Taranaki's early days when wars with the Maoris seemed to go on and on for years. Life must have been traumatic for the women living in outlying districts.'

His brows drew together as his hands dropped to his sides. 'Are you saying you wouldn't have followed the man you loved?'

Lisa knew he was watching her closely, but she returned his gaze unflinchingly. 'I would have expected the man I loved to have had a little consideration for me—to think twice before placing me in such danger. And apart from living in terror of the Maories there were bush fires to contend with.'

'Plenty of women stood up to the troubles and trials of those days,' he said pointedly. 'Naturally, it took guts.' His voice held a tinge of derision.

'No doubt.' She forced herself to remain cool. 'But

you must remember that those men went into the back country because it was something *they* wanted to do. The women had little or no option. At that period they were mere chattels who followed their men like blind idiots, suffering all kinds of privations because that was what the men not only expected, but demanded.'

Brett gave a short laugh. 'You've sure got your knife into some of those fellows!'

'It's the thought of the inequality that annoys me. It was a man's world, and some of them were mighty inconsiderate—but that was before Women's Lib raised its courageous head.'

'You're giving three cheers for Women's Lib?'

'Definitely. As I read this book I can't help thinking of those poor pioneer women, many with hungry children, running out of food until the next bullock wagon arrived from New Plymouth—some with sick children and no doctor within miles, others walking through the dark bush to help each other in childbirth——'

She stopped for breath and fell silent, her jaw dropping slightly as a thought struck her with sudden force. The root of it had been her own words, and it caused her to get up and move restlessly about the room, then pause beside the fireplace where she stared into the flames while it developed in her mind.

Brett watched her intently. 'What's going on in that head of yours? You look as though you've been hit by an inspiration.'

'Yes, I have—I think.'

'Well, out with it. I'll tell you if it's a good one.'

She looked at him doubtfully. 'I should discuss it with Catherine first. It's her book—and her decision.'

'Are you sure it's her decision? I thought you're supposed to be editing this manuscript.'

'I mean it's for her to decide whether or not she'll follow the idea through. It may not appeal to her.'

He became exasperated. 'Will you please tell me

what you have in mind—or must I shake it out of you?'

'It's the stories about the women, coupled with all the trivia which mainly concern the women,' Lisa explained. 'Lift it all out and the manuscript would be relieved of many thousands of words, on top of which Catherine would have a second book.'

He was looking at her with new respect. 'By Jove, I think you've come up with an excellent idea! I'm beginning to believe you really do know your job.'

'Are you saying you doubted it?' she laughed, glowing beneath his praise, then she brushed it aside as she said, 'Apart from everything else those pioneer women deserved to be remembered.'

'You're right, and I can just see Catherine getting her teeth into this lot. She's spent ages trying to think of a subject for another book, and now you've come up with this idea!' He made an impulsive mmovement and again grabbed her by the shoulders, staring down into her face as he held her against his chest.

A shiver of delight slithered down Lisa's spine and her heart began to thud as she waited for the feel of his lips on her own. Somehow she felt it would be a kiss that was long and gently passionate—a kiss that would tell her she was becoming someone of importance in his life.

Brett held her for several moments, almost as though waiting for her to protest and push against his chest, but when she failed to do so his arms tightened about her body until his hands began a quietly sensuous movement as they massaged the muscles of her back.

Slowly she raised her face, inviting his kiss, but to her intense surprise and utter chagrin it did not come. His lips did not find hers, and instead of the passion she longed for he merely rested his cheek against her forehead in a gesture that was little more than brotherly.

A vague feeling of having been snubbed niggled at her, and she almost felt herself go pale as she realised he'd *known* she'd been waiting for his caress. Anger with herself more than with him caused her to twist and escape from his arms, and she crossed the room to stare unseeingly through the window. She had been there only a few moments before Mary came into the room.

Brett said mildly, 'I thought I heard a car door slam. I guessed you'd arrived home.' And although he spoke to Mary his eyes glinted wickedly as they sent Lisa a mocking glance.

His teasing explanation sent a flush to her cheeks, then her attention was caught by the unexpected sight of Mary's sparkling eyes and glowing face. The change made her look quite lovely.

Nor was her radiant appearance lost upon Brett. 'Where have you been?' he demanded quietly, his eyes raking her face.

'Oh, into Eltham and then on to Stratford. I did some shopping and saw a few friends,' she added carelessly.

'Are you trying to tell me you haven't spent the whole day with Paul?' Brett demanded suspiciously.

'What makes you think so?' she retorted, on the defensive.

'Because it's written all over your face. Come on, admit it!'

'Okay, suppose I *have* been with Paul? Since when have I had to account for my movements to you, big brother?'

'Since the day you were born—or almost,' he snapped. 'You were at his house, I presume?'

'So what? We had a lot to talk about.' She sent a quietly triumphant smile towards Lisa as she added, 'We were making *plans*.'

'Indeed? What sort of plans?' Brett queried, frowning.

'Mind your own flaming business!' Mary snapped defiantly, and ran from the room.

Lisa's finely drawn brows arched as she looked at him. 'I must say your attitude surprises me. I thought that this was an association you were trying to encourage, but now you sound as though you're no longer pleased about Mary becoming close to Paul.'

The scowl still darkened his brow. 'I'm damned if I know what to think. I must admit I was uneasy about him from the beginning, but I pushed those doubts aside because I could see Mary was keen on him. However, some of your remarks concerning him have now stirred the misgivings I had in the first instance.' He was silent for several minutes before he added, 'I'd be interested to learn more about their plans—whatever they are.'

Lisa also felt an interest in their plans, although she was assailed by a feeling of unease because, from the little she had seen of them together, she did not really believe that Paul was in love with Mary. Further, it would have surprised her if the plans concerned marriage.

But what could she herself say or do about the situation? As Brett had said, she had already dropped several warning hints about Paul, but she now decided that in future she would mind her own business. Silence would be her golden rule.

In the meantime she was anxious to discuss her own plan concerning the women in Catherine's book, but the opportunity to do so did not arise until during dinner that evening. Nor did it take Catherine more than a few seconds to grasp and understand Lisa's idea. Her eyes shone as she thought of it.

'It's splendid—I like it,' she exclaimed happily. 'I've been trying to find a subject for another book, and there it was, right under my nose!'

'It'll mean more research,' Lisa warned. 'The women already in the book will have to be extended, and you'll have to find others to go with them. A manuscript of about eighty thousand words should be sufficient.'

'I'll do it.' Catherine was full of enthusiasm.

'It will also mean that my job with *Mountain Memory* will be made much shorter and easier,' Lisa pointed out. 'It'll enable me to get rid of thousands of words in less time. Your brother was right when he said there was more than one book in the manuscript.'

Mary looked at her in sudden dismay. 'Does that mean you'll go home sooner than expected?'

Lisa felt a sense of surprise. 'Naturally, if it shortens the work—although I find it hard to believe that you'll be sorry to see me go home.'

'Yes, actually, perhaps I shall.' Mary looked down at her plate, her disappointment obvious, and an evasiveness about her that made Lisa look at her thoughtfully.

'Would you like to come home with me?' asked Lisa. 'The invitation is still open, you know.'

'No, thank you, I have other plans.' The words came hastily.

'So you said before,' Brett said dryly. 'Why don't you tell us about them? What exactly are these plans?'

'They're my own business,' Mary retorted stubbornly.

Watching her, Lisa was again puzzled, and as the evening wore on she became filled with the conviction that, for some strange reason, Mary was *not* anxious to see her return to the North Shore. To put this thought to the test she referred to her work by saying casually. 'I'm afraid it'll be ages and ages before I'm *really* finished with *Mountain Memory*.'

The words caused Mary to brighten visibly and Lisa knew that her suspicion had been correct. Nor was the reason difficult to fathom. Hadn't Paul said something about finding a job on the North Shore? And with herself at home did Mary fear he would be lost to her? But what were the 'plans' she had referred to?

The rest of the week passed quickly, with Lisa spending her days in the library. When she began work at eight-thirty each morning the woodbox was always filled, the fire was burning brightly, but there was never a sign of Brett. Even during lunchtime he was seldom in the house.

At morning and afternoon tea breaks the need for exercise sent her outside to take a quick walk round the garden and along the drive, where the umbrella fronds of the tall tree-ferns never ceased to fascinate her. And while she was taking these walks her eyes scanned every direction for the sight of Brett, but apart from the faint sound of the farm motorbike in the distance there was little or no sign of him. Was he deliberately avoiding her?

With the exception of Tuesdays she was usually paid a short visit by Gwen Yates who came in to dust the library. Short and plump, Gwen was quick and capable, and as she cleaned the glass of the French door she said, 'The garden beside this veranda is beautiful in the spring. You'll love it when the tulips are out.'

Lisa smiled, 'I doubt that I'll be here in the spring.'

Gwen's round face registered surprise. 'You won't? I thought you'd come to stay.'

'Only until this job is completed.'

'Well, blow me down! I thought you and Mr Arlington——' Her voice trailed off as she fell silent.

Lisa sat back and looked at her. 'What about Mr Arlington and me, Gwen?'

Gwen swallowed, then mumbled, 'Nothing— nothing at all. It was just something I thought Mrs Arlington said. Maybe I was mistaken.'

'Lots of people make mistakes, Gwen, one of the most foolish being to indulge in wishful thinking. It gets one nowhere.' Lisa sighed as she bent her head over the papers on the table.

The days continued to pass, with little communication between Brett and herself. Nor was this unsociable attitude any different from his demeanour during the evenings, when he watched television for only a short time before disappearing from the lounge.

Catherine made excuses for him. 'Brett has never allowed himself to become enslaved by the goggle-box. He likes to read in the evenings, so if you want him you'll find him in the library. If he's not reading he'll be attending to his farm accounts.'

Lisa felt a sense of relief. At least it wasn't her own presence that was driving him from the room, as she'd begun to fear.

The following Tuesday Brett happened to be making one of his rare lunchtime appearances when Catherine turned to Lisa and said,

'I'm going to the Eltham Country Women's Institute meeting at two o'clock. It's a special afternoon, with a display of wool work put on by a spinning and weaving group from Hawera. Would you like to take time off to come and see it?'

Lisa shook her head. 'No, thank you—I wouldn't be taking the afternoon off in Auckland, so I shan't do it here.'

Brett glanced at his sister, then spoke to Catherine. 'Is Mary going with you? She should be mixing with more people.'

Catherine gave a slight shrug. 'I've asked her to come, but she isn't keen.' The look she sent him said more than her words.

Brett turned to Mary. 'Why not? You might be interested in learning to do some of this wool work.'

Mary's expression was sullen. 'Couldn't you hear? As Catherine has already told you, I'm not keen.'

'At least the outing would do you good,' he persisted. 'It might help to shake off that morose attitude I've noticed recently. It's been sitting on your shoulders like a cloak of doom.'

Mary's only reply was to leave the table with what sounded suspiciously like a stifled sob.

'What the hell's the matter with her?' Brett demanded crossly.

'I'm afraid it must be Paul,' Catherine admitted reluctantly. 'I don't think she's seen very much of him recently.'

'But I understand there are plans in the air,' he pursued.

Catherine shook her head, then whispered, 'If there are she's being very cagey about them. I've certainly been told nothing, so perhaps they've collapsed. I hope he's not building false hopes.'

'All the more reason for her to become interested in a hobby of some sort,' Brett growled. 'See if you can persuade her to go to the Institute with you. I think it's important.'

Catherine did her best, and Mary eventually agreed to accompany her to the meeting—and as Gwen did not go to the homestead on Tuesdays Lisa found herself alone in the house. For a short time she became conscious of the country silence, broken only by the occasional bellow from a cow or bleat of a sheep, but by the middle of the afternoon she was working steadily, her mind busy with paragraphs that needed re-wording to give the same information in less space.

Sun filtered into the room where the only sounds came from the rustling of paper, the ticking of the clock or the movement of a log flaring in the fireplace. And then the sound of a step on the veranda caught her ear.

She paused, pen in hand, but did not look round. So Brett had at last seen fit to come and talk to her. In that case he needn't expect a show of delighted surprise on her part. She heard a tap on the glass, the turning of the door handle, and only then did she turn round. But it wasn't Brett who stepped into the room—it was Paul Mason.

Lisa glared at him in blank dismay, then demanded angrily, 'What are you doing here? You've no right to walk in uninvited!'

'Who cares about rights?' he grinned. 'I knocked on the back door in case Gwen Yates was here, but there was no reply. Anyhow, I guessed you were alone because I saw Catherine and Mary in Eltham.' His light blue eyes glanced towards the garden. 'Where's Brett?'

'I've no idea,' she snapped, then immediately regretted the words, wishing she'd said that Brett was somewhere close at hand.

'He's probably away to hell at the back of the farm, or climbing old Egmont,' Paul surmised knowingly. 'I doubt that he'll disturb us while we have a talk. It's about time we got things clear.'

'What do you mean? There's nothing to get clear.'

'Don't fool yourself, Lisa. I want to know why the devil you ran out on me and why you didn't bother to answer my letters. Even when I tried to phone you hung up on me.'

'Don't bother to lie, Paul. You know exactly why I wanted a clean break between us. The last time I spoke to you I explained that Maggie Simpson's face would always come between us. Surely that was clear enough.'

'But I loved you——'

She shook her head. 'You didn't love me at all. I was merely a challenge, someone you were aiming to get to bed.'

'I was sure you loved me,' he persisted.

'I thought so too, until I lost all respect for you. By the way, how is Maggie? And the little boy? Where are they?'

His face twisted with anger. 'That stupid, simpering, whining twit——'

'Yes, that same Maggie whom you betrayed and left to fend for herself, to go through the trauma of giving birth to *your* son, and who now bears the burden of bringing him up.' Lisa discovered she was shaking with anger.

'Dammit, I pay maintenance for him,' he snarled defensively.

'I should damned well think you would!' she retorted heatedly. 'Now, if you don't mind, I'd like to get on with my work, so *goodbye*.' She turned again to the papers on the table.

Paul gave a short laugh. 'If you think you can give me the brush-off as easily as that, you can think again!'

She looked at him earnestly. 'You're making a mistake, Paul. Apart from the odd polite remark I don't want to have anything to do with you. Surely that's plain enough?'

'Not to me, it isn't.' His face had become mutinous.

She was puzzled. 'What do you mean?' Then, exasperated, she indicated the pages of manuscript. 'Look at all this—I've a big job on hand and I'd be grateful if you'd let me get on with it. So will you please leave?'

'Can't you see? That's the whole point. The fact that you've come here to do this job can't be a mere fluke. Even I, with my lack of knowledge about the publishing world, can guess that a job such as this would normally be done in the office. You evidently knew I was living next door, even if it's several fields away.'

Lisa looked at him in silence. Dear God, she thought, his mind is following the same trend as Brett's! 'Are you suggesting I came here because of you?' she asked at last.

'Of course you did. It's obvious. I knew it at once.'

'You're entirely mistaken,' she snapped angrily. 'The circumstances surrounding this book are different from others, nor do I intend explaining them to you. And let me assure you it was Catherine who arranged for me to do the job here. If I'd known you were living so close I wouldn't have set foot near the place.'

'Come on, Lisa, you can't fool me. You're playing a little game of being hard to get.'

Her eyes narrowed slightly as she looked at him thoughtfully. 'You'd like us to take up where we left off, huh?'

He grinned. 'Now you're talking sense!'

'Have you forgotten Mary? What about her?' Her blue eyes were accusing as she awaited his answer.

'Mary?' he shrugged. 'I've no commitment with Mary in any way.'

'I understand that you have plans for the future.'

His sandy brows drew together. 'Plans? What are you talking about? What plans did she mention?'

'Don't try and dodge the issue. I'm talking about the plans you have with Mary.' Curiosity made her prevaricate. 'I'd have to hear about them from you before I'd—er—consider anything.'

His face cleared. 'Oh, *those* plans. They're nothing. You can forget about them.'

'I don't think Mary's forgotten about them. When they were first made they were important enough to send her over the moon.'

'They were really all *her* ideas, not my idea at all——'

'I'm listening,' Lisa encouraged.

'Very well. It was after I'd had Sunday night's tea here when I spoke of finding a job in Auckland. Do you remember?'

She nodded, then said, 'You'd like one with an accountant on the North Shore. You want to be close to the boating and swimming?'

He looked at her meaningfully. 'That's only one of the reasons. Well, Mary tackled me about it next day, wanting to know where I'd live. I told her I'd find a flat somewhere, then added jokingly that I'd have to find a good cook, someone who could make a nice fish pie. I'm afraid she jumped to the conclusion that I meant her, and she took it as an invitation to move in with me.'

Lisa was appalled. 'Brett would never allow it! He'd have your kidneys for breakfast—your guts for garters!'

'You're forgetting she's an adult and can please herself,' Paul pointed out coldly.

'And for how long would she continue to please *you*?' Lisa queried shrewdly. 'You and your reputation?'

He shrugged. 'I don't know. Frankly, she can be a bit of a bore. She's not like you—vivid and alive.'

She ignored the compliment. 'Then you're not contemplating marriage with Mary?'

He was shocked. '*Marriage?* Hell, no—who said anything about marriage? Would I be wanting you back if I were?'

'I suppose not. Well, this has been most interesting. Now will you *please go*? This is the third time of asking.'

'Okay, so you'll come out with me tonight?'

'Not tonight, nor any other night. Goodbye, Paul.'

'What the hell—I thought we were getting along nicely.'

'Did you indeed? Then you'll have to learn to think much more clearly.' She turned away from him and again bent over her work.

Paul's eyes glittered with anger as he stepped closer to sweep the papers across the table, grab her arm and jerk her to her feet. Twisting her round to face him, he gritted, 'Then you're saying it really is finished between us?'

'*Finished!* For heaven's sake, Paul, it finished three years ago. You're mighty slow to grasp the situation.'

'Slow, am I? I'm not too slow for this——' His arms snatched her to him, holding her in a firm grip. 'At least you'll kiss me again. I reckon I can arouse you——'

# HARLEQUIN READER SERVICE

## ⊷§ FREE OFFER CARD §⊶

**PLACE HEART STICKER HERE**

**FREE PEN AND WATCH SET**

**4 FREE BOOKS**

**FREE HOME DELIVERY**

**PLUS AN EXTRA BONUS "MYSTERY GIFT"!**

☐ YES! Please send me my four HARLEQUIN ROMANCES® books, free, along with my free Pen and Watch Set and Mystery Gift! Then send me six new HARLEQUIN ROMANCES books every month, as they come off the presses, and bill me at just $1.66 per book (29¢ less than retail), with no extra charges for shipping and handling. If I am not completely satisfied, I may return a shipment and cancel at any time. The free books, Pen, Watch and Mystery Gift remain mine to keep!

116 CIR EAX5

FIRST NAME_____ LAST NAME_____
(PLEASE PRINT)

ADDRESS_____ APT._____

CITY_____

PROV./STATE_____ POSTAL CODE/ZIP_____

PRINTED IN U.S.A.

BUSINESS REPLY CARD

First Class    Permit No. 717    Buffalo, NY

Postage will be paid by addressee

*Harlequin Reader Service*

901 Fuhrmann Blvd.,

P.O. Box 1394

Buffalo, NY 14240-9963

NO POSTAGE
NECESSARY
IF MAILED
IN THE
UNITED STATES

'Go to hell!' she shrieked in fury, struggling against his strength. 'No, I won't kiss you—get your hands off me!'

His grip held her firmly. 'Surely you'll kiss me goodbye in a civilised manner?'

She became still. 'Only if you really mean goodbye.' It would be worth it to be rid of him, she decided.

'Yes, I mean it. After this I'll never bother you again.'

'You promise—faithfully?'

'I promise. Cross my heart and hope to die.'

'And no more of your subtle remarks calculated to make Mary jealous,' she persisted. 'They not only make her jealous, they also hurt her deeply.'

Paul's grin was satanic. 'She could do with a bit of stirring up!'

'You evidently get pleasure out of hurting people, Paul,' Lisa said coldly. 'Does it feed your ego, or does it give you a sense of power?'

'A little of both, I think,' he admitted blatantly.

She felt disgusted. 'Can we get this stupidity over?' she snapped. 'Then you can go.'

She raised her face, but his kiss left her cold. The touch of his lips no longer had the power to stir her blood and she found it impossible to respond in any way. It was also impossible to understand why she had thought she had been in love with him three years ago, and she could only put it down to immaturity.

'You've become cold,' he accused as he released her.

'To you, I have—so now you know. And if you dare to break your promise to me I'll tell Mary about Maggie Simpson.' She looked at him reproachfully. 'I don't suppose you ever bother to see how she's faring.'

'She's all right,' he muttered sulkily. 'She's working in a waterfront motel where everyone she meets soon learns that the father of her boy is named Paul Mason. She's even had the temerity to have the boy baptised Paul Mason Simpson.'

'Poor Maggie,' Lisa said softly.

His mouth twisted slightly as he looked at her in silence for several moments while she prayed he would leave. But at last he said, 'I'll let myself out through the back door. My car's in the yard.'

She listened as the sound of his heavy footsteps faded along the passage, then knew an immense relief as she heard the slam of the back door. Would he keep his promise to leave her alone? She could only hope so.

Feeling suddenly relaxed, she bent over the table to straighten the papers he had swept into disorderly array, and as she began to stack them a sound came from behind her. She turned to face Brett, who had come in by the French doors, his face grim with accusation.

He watched in silence as she continued to straighten the papers, and when he spoke his voice was heavy with sarcasm. 'I see you've had a visitor. Interrupted your work, did he?'

The derision in his voice filled her with an inward horror. Had he just arrived or had he witnessed——? Yes, of course he had. From the look of condemnation on his face it seemed obvious he had spent several minutes on the veranda—watching her being kissed by Paul.

# CHAPTER SIX

THE knowledge that Brett had observed Paul embracing her filled Lisa with dismay, but she made a determined effort to treat the matter casually and as if it were of no consequence.

'Yes, Paul was here,' she admitted lightly. 'No doubt you saw him leaving?' There was a tremor of hope in the question. Perhaps, after all, Brett had merely seen him driving away.

But Brett's next words dashed this spark of optimism. 'Not exactly. I was crossing the lawn on my way to see you when I realised he was in here, so I waited until he'd gone. I must say the last few minutes were most touching, to say nothing of being revealing.' His lip curled with derision.

'Then you'll have heard what was said?' She was still hopeful.

'No. The door was closed, but I could see into the room, and let me tell you that watching was more than enough without hearing all your endearments as well,' he gritted.

'That's a pity,' she said quietly. 'You might have learnt enough to clear your mind.'

'I can assure you there was no need to hear a word,' he retorted coldly. 'The view from the veranda was sufficient. I must say you had me well and truly fooled, Lisa.'

She recoiled from the disgust on his face. 'Fooled? What—what do you mean?'

'Can't you work it out for yourself? he snarled. 'You've been adamant in your assertion that your affair with Paul ended three years ago, and that you had no idea he was our neighbour—yet I find you in his arms. I presume you rang and told him you'd be alone this afternoon.'

'Wrong. Your presumption, as well as the rest of your conclusions, are way off base.'

'Do you expect me to believe that? With Catherine and Mary nicely out of the house, and Gwen not here on Tuesdays, it was a golden opportunity to see him alone. Why did you have to go about it in such a sneaky manner?' His voice rang with scorn.

'*Sneaky!* How *dare* you apply that term to me!' Lisa's face had paled. Her temper bubbled, but she fought to keep it under control, although she knew she was beginning to shake.

'Why can't you be honest and admit you phoned him?' Brett hammered at her in a fury.

'Because I *didn't*, that's why!' she shouted.

'A liar as well!' he lashed at her, his disgust obvious.

Her chin rose and her tone grew icy as she took a grip on herself. 'Would you please allow me to get on with this job? I'm longing to get it finished so that I can get to hell out of your house. That day can't come soon enough for me!'

'A fact I can well believe, now that Paul has ideas of finding a job of some sort on the North Shore,' he sneered.

'Believe what you like,' Lisa snapped furiously as she turned away and sat at the table, her heart heavy with depression.

But even after Brett had left the room she found concentration almost impossible. *A sneak and a liar,* he'd called her. The words were still ringing in her ears. Tears sprang to her eyes and were dashed away angrily. Why on earth was she allowing him to get under her skin in this manner? Why should she care what he thought of her?

Yet she knew she *did* care—deeply. Nor could she tolerate the knowledge that he regarded her as a sneak and a liar. It sent a horrible pain coursing through her entire being, and again the pages became blurred as the tears welled into her eyes and rolled down her cheeks.

Frustrated by the uncontrolled tumult raging in her mind, she felt a sudden urge for fresh air, so, laying down her pen, she went out through the French doors and began to walk about the garden. Marigolds and chrysanthemums were still making a brave show of gold and bronze, but she hardly saw them, and even the late afternoon sun turning the liquid-ambered autumn leaves to a brilliant maze of scarlet, crimson and yellow failed to attract her attention.

Standing beneath the colourful tree, she gazed towards the high mountain. 'What's the matter with me, Taranaki?' she whispered, with none but herself to hear. 'I should be loathing him, but I'm not. I should be packing up right now and hurrying home to Auckland to finish the job in the office, yet in all honesty, I can't bear to leave this place. When I leave Lynton I'll never see him again—*I'll never see him again*. Why should it hurt so much? Can you tell me that, Taranaki? Surely I'm not in love with him. *Or am I?*'

It was then that the revelation came, shocking her like an earth-moving jolt. The scene about her faded to a blur until even the mountain's bulk disappeared and she saw only the face of one man—the dark eyes, the firm mouth and jaw of Brett Arlington.

'Is it true, Taranaki?' she whispered, still gazing towards the mountain. 'Do I really love him?' But even if it had been possible, there was no need for the mountain to reply, because she knew the truth without a shadow of doubt, and she also knew the fact must be kept hidden at all costs. The thought of one who scorned her knowing she loved him made her cringe inwardly.

She didn't see Brett again until Catherine served the evening meal, and he was then only distantly polite.

Not that his remote attitude towards her was noticeable, because conversation at the table was dominated by Catherine's enthusiastic description of the woolcraft displayed at the Institute meeting by the Hawera spinning and weaving group.

'Beautiful garments—blankets, wall hangings and floor mats,' she exclaimed. 'And also a demonstration as well, because they'd brought their looms and spinning wheels. One of the women had borrowed her husband's farm truck, and I can tell you it was piled high!' She turned to Mary who had been sitting in silence. 'Didn't you think those homespun cardigans and jerseys were attractive?'

Mary was startled, her mind appearing to be elsewhere. 'What—? Oh yes, lovely and warm,' she agreed half-heartedly.

'Now that's something you could take up,' Catherine pursued. 'Would you like to learn to spin? We've got our own wool growing almost at the back door—some lovely fleeces on the younger sheep.'

But Mary was not interested. 'Oh no, I don't think so.' She gave a small shudder. 'I wouldn't like handling the raw wool from the shorn sheep—it's so— so smelly and greasy.'

'Greasy? My dear, that's pure lanolin,' Catherine assured her.

Mary turned to Lisa, a question on her lips, her brown eyes anxious yet full of hope. 'Did the phone ring this afternoon? Was there a call for me—from anyone?'

Lisa knew she was really asking if Paul had rung. 'No, there were no phone calls, either inward or outward,' she declared firmly, her direct gaze including Brett as well as Mary.

He returned her stare mockingly, his dark eyes accusing and plainly saying the word *liar*.

She also realised he was waiting for her to admit to Mary that Paul had come to the house that afternoon, but she decided against it because it would involve too much explanation. In any case, Mary's question had concerned phone calls rather than visitors, and it would only add to her disappointment to know that Paul had been there during her absence.

Further, if Brett insisted upon regarding her as a sneak and a liar, her pride would not allow her to plead with him to believe otherwise. She could only hope the time would come when he'd believe otherwise.

That evening there was little of interest on television. Brett sat glowering at it for a short time, his long form stretched in an armchair, while Lisa watched him covertly from beneath her lashes. But at last, almost as though he knew he was being observed, he got up and left the room.

His departure made the lounge seem empty, and, using the poor programme as an excuse, Lisa told Catherine she would like to do some work on the manuscript. She didn't admit she had had a disrupted afternoon, but this had been a fact, and she felt she would like to make up for lost time. However, when she reached the library she found Brett sitting at the desk and busy with accounts.

He turned as she entered, then, seeing her hesitate and about to leave, he rasped, 'Come in—I want to talk to you.'

The coldness in his voice struck a chill to her bones. 'More discussion about Paul, I suppose?'

'How did you guess?' His voice dripped sarcasm. 'Don't you think it's time you came clean and explained to Mary the true situation between Paul and yourself?'

'What, in your opinion, is the true situation?'

'It's obvious you're taking up where you left off three years ago. She'll be upset, of course, but she'll get over it. Better to have a small hurt now than a much larger one later.'

Lisa gave a sigh of exasperation. 'Haven't I made it clear that as far as Paul is concerned, Mary has nothing to fear from me?'

'And didn't I see you in his arms? The kiss I witnessed wasn't a mere brush on the cheek, it was passionate.' His lip curled.

She looked at him helplessly. 'It's a pity you couldn't have overheard our previous conversation. I'll admit he came to see *me*, and not Mary.'

'Ah, then no doubt you'll also admit you rang him.'

Her voice rose. '*I did not ring him!* Why don't you believe me?'

'How can I believe anything you say if you'll lie over something as small as a phone call?'

'For Pete's sake, how can I get it through to you that I'm telling you the *truth*? Really, I can't take any more of this——'

Tears pricked her lids, but before her eyes could fill she went to the table, snatched up a chapter, her scribbling pad and a ballpoint pen. But before she could hurry from the room Brett jumped to his feet and grabbed her arm.

'Lisa, I want to believe you, but every time I try I get a vision of you in Paul's arms, your face raised while he kisses you. Nor did I notice any struggles of protest from you.'

She wrenched her arm free of his hand. 'No. There was a reason for that,' she told him stonily. 'Good night. I'll do some work in bed.' And with that she hurried from the room.

It was his lack of faith in her that hurt most of all, she realised, and then, as she sat up in bed, the desire to work eluded her as the tears fell and the words became blurred. It was also an effort to concentrate, but at last she succeeded, and it was almost midnight when she switched off the bedside lamp. Her tears then soaked into the pillow, and as Brett's accusation began a rhythmic beat in her brain recollection of the words *liar* and *sneak* made her want to scream with frustration.

Nor did she sleep well. The emotional stress and late work had caused a restlessness that left her feeling anything but refreshed next morning. However, a hot shower helped to revive her, and when she went to the kitchen she found Catherine, Mary and Brett already sitting at breakfast.

Catherine's sharp eyes examined her face. 'You look as if you worked late. There's no need for it, unless you're in a hurry to leave us. Now sit down and have a good breakfast—ah, here's Gwen. What a blessing she is!'

Gwen came in through the back door, a smock over her round figure showing she was ready for work.

Catherine greeted her cheerfully, then said, 'I didn't see you at the Institute yesterday. Isn't it something you never miss?'

'Indeed it is,' Gwen declared almost wrathfully. 'Please don't remind me I wasn't there.'

'Yesterday was something special,' Catherine enthused. 'The Hawera spinning and weaving people put on a wonderful display of their work. You'd have been most interested, especially as you're such a good spinner. Actually, I was wondering if you'd teach Mary to spin. I'm sure it's something she could learn——'

'I don't want to learn to spin,' Mary interrupted crossly. 'You're not going to manipulate *me*, Catherine!' she flared, glaring at her stepmother.

Catherine ignored the outburst. 'All right, dear, perhaps at some other time.' Then, turning to Gwen, 'But really, I was so sorry when I realised you weren't there, because I know you'd have been most interested.'

Gwen began to stack the dishes on the sink bench. 'I missed it because I was anxious about my sister who lives in Inglewood,' she explained. 'She hasn't been well for weeks and I ring her every few days to see if she's making an improvement. She's changed her doctor and is on new pills, and I wanted to know if they were making a difference—but when I discovered the dratted phone was out of order I had no option but to drive to Inglewood to see her condition for myself.'

Brett put his cup down slowly, then turned to look at Gwen. 'I presume you mean your own phone, Gwen? John didn't mention it.'

'They were out all over the district—Paul Mason's, yours—everyone's. Didn't you know?'

'You mean they were out of action only in the morning?'

'No, they were out all day until about four in the afternoon,' Gwen declared in aggrieved tones. 'It took the linesmen ages to find the trouble.'

'Are you sure about this, Gwen?' Brett persisted.

She swept him a glance of surprise. 'Sure? It caused me to miss the Institute meeting, didn't it? You can bet I'm sure!'

Brett did not pursue the subject, and although Lisa watched him steadily in an effort to catch his eye the brief glance he sent her revealed nothing of his thoughts.

Later, when she was working in the library he came into the room and stood beside the mantelpiece. She forced herself to keep her head down, although she was well aware that he stood with his back to the fireplace, his long muscled legs astride, and his arms folded across his broad chest. When he spoke his words came as a surprise, causing her to look at him.

'Okay, so I'm ready to believe you didn't ring Paul Mason.'

'You are? That's mighty big of you. Thank you for nothing!' She turned away again.

'I'm trying to tell you, I no longer consider you to be a liar.'

'Is that a fact? It must be difficult for you to admit it,' she returned quietly, her eyes shadowed to the darkness of sapphires.

'No doubt I wasn't thinking very clearly,' he admitted. 'You can put it down to a blinding rage. Do you understand?'

'Perfectly. You were annoyed because you saw your sister's so-called boy-friend kissing me. That I can understand.'

'There's more to it than that,' Brett retorted enigmatically.

'Oh yes, there's my *sneakiness* to be accounted for. That's another charming trait you added to my character!'

His mouth became grim. 'While we're on the subject perhaps you could clear up that point.'

'Are you asking in what sneaky manner did I manage to get him here, considering the phone was out of order?' Lisa queried with a hint of reproach.

'No, I'm not asking that at all—but you said Paul had come to see you, rather than Mary. Why would he do that?'

'Because he wanted to talk to me—privately. He knew that neither Catherine nor Mary were home because he happened to see them in Eltham. I can tell you his arrival gave me a shock.'

'So—he wanted to talk to you. What about?'

She gave a slight shrug. 'I doubt that you'd be interested.'

'Try me and see.' He left the mantelpiece to stand beside her.

'It's really no concern of yours.'

'Can't you understand that I'm making it my concern?'

Lisa looked at him doubtfully, wondering if she should tell him the truth. Perhaps it would be better, she decided. Perhaps it would clear the air between them and lead to a better understanding, so she said,

'Actually he—he tried to persuade me to continue our old relationship, to take up where we'd left off.'

'I didn't realise you'd been engaged to him.' His eyes held a strange glitter that puzzled her.

'I was *not* engaged to him—but I *thought* I was about to be given a ring,' she admitted. 'Instead I went off home to Auckland. Paul now pretends he couldn't understand my reason for doing so.'

'Well, what made you do it?'

'I'd lost respect for him. I realised I wasn't the only love in his life—I was just one of several. Mary is now in the same position, although she's unable to believe it.'

'You've warned her about him?'

'I've dropped hints, but so far they've had no effect. Naturally, it's something she doesn't want to know about, so I'm afraid it's something she'll have to learn for herself. People seldom alter very much, and I'm sure Paul will go through life telling himself it's time for a change.'

Brett said with an edge to his voice, 'It's a pity Mary couldn't have seen you in his arms, as I did. I still consider that embrace needs a little explaining.'

'Not really,' Lisa shrugged. 'It was merely a goodbye kiss for his promise not to pester me again. Or are you having difficulty in believing me?' she flared with a sudden burst of vexation.

He looked at her searchingly. 'My word, you *are* tired and irritable this morning!'

'I know exactly how I feel,' she snapped. 'Yesterday upset me more than you realise, what with being called sneaky and a liar!'

'It's obviously something you'll neither forget nor forgive.'

She looked at him in silence, longing to admit she was willing to do both. At the same time a lump in her throat warned that tears were near. Lack of sleep and the emotional strain of the last few hours were beginning to take their toll, and she felt drained. The sensation of weakness that came over her made her yearn to go to him, to put her arms about him while she leaned against him and lifted her face for his kiss— but to do so was unthinkable. And then his voice hit her ears.

'Okay, so I'll get out of your sight.'

As he moved towards the door she knew she didn't want him to leave, and, pulling herself together mentally, she made an effort to delay him. 'Brett——' she began.

He swung round to face her. 'Yes?'

'Yesterday you said you were crossing the lawn to see me——'

'Yes. I was coming in to tell you I intended taking you up to Dawson Falls on Saturday. Naturally, when I saw you in Paul Mason's arms I presumed you wouldn't want to come with me.' He paused, looking at her in silence for several moments before he asked, 'Do you want to come? You don't have to if you're beginning to hate my guts. I'll quite understand.' His mouth took on the grim line she was beginning to recognise.

'Oh yes, thank you, I'd like to come.' A surge of excitement shot through her, making it difficult to hide her eagerness.

'Right. We'll leave on Saturday morning and have lunch up at the Tourist Lodge. Weather permitting, of course.'

Lisa's heart lifted, the depression vanished, and for the rest of the day she found no difficulty in putting her mind to her work. And as the next few days passed she was gripped by a fever of hopeful expectancy that caused her pen to fly as she pruned and rewrote some of Catherine's long, wordy paragraphs.

Saturday came at last, and when Lisa woke she was conscious of an inner exhilaration—nor did she try to deny that it was caused by the anticipation of Brett taking her to Dawson Falls. Springing out of bed, she drew back the curtains, to discover the lawn white and glistening with frost, the sky cloudless and giving promise of a clear and sunny day. She showered quickly, took special care with her make-up and put on her warm royal blue track-suit because she guessed the air would be crisp and chilly up on the mountain.

When she went into the kitchen she half expected to see Mary wearing her tan track-suit and ready to accompany them, but instead she was neatly dressed in her brown jersey and pleated skirt, which was not the best attire for scrambling along mountain tracks.

'Aren't you coming with us?' asked Lisa.

Mary smiled complacently. 'No, thank you. I've been up to the Falls and the Tourist Lodge many times.' Then, with a light of quiet satisfaction in her eyes, she said, 'Paul is coming to take me to Stratford. We're to have lunch with Tom and Beryl Walker. Beryl has just had her first baby,' she explained to Lisa. 'We were best friends at school. I was her bridesmaid and she'll be my matron of honour when——' She stopped abruptly, a flush staining her cheeks as she realised what she had been about to say.

'Are you hinting you've had a proposal of marriage?' Brett demanded sharply.

Mary's flush deepened. 'Well, as good as——' she muttered defiantly but without meeting his eyes.

His gaze narrowed slightly as it rested upon his sister. 'Is this the *plan* you referred to?'

'You'll know when the time comes,' she retorted.

Lisa came to Mary's rescue by turning to Catherine. 'You're not coming with us?'

Catherine shook her head. 'Definitely not. There are several jobs I'd like to get out of the way before I start thinking about the book on early women. You and Brett will have a lovely day together. I'm sure it'll prove to be a perfect one for you both, one you'll always remember.' There was a speculative gleam in the hazel eyes as they moved from Lisa to Brett.

Lisa felt herself go hot and was unable to look at Brett. Had he caught the calculating expression Catherine had made no attempt to hide? She found herself groping for words. 'Yes, I'm sure you're right. The sky's so clear and—and a fine day usually follows a frost,' she finished lamely.

'Never judge the day by the morning,' Catherine warned. 'That's an old Chinese proverb. The mountain draws the rain, and up on the slopes the weather can change at the drop of a hat. The clouds gather and the mist seems to arrive from out of nowhere. But you need have no fear of getting lost, because Brett will be with you. He'll take good care of you.' She smiled knowingly.

Brett stood up abruptly, the sudden movement causing his chair to scrape the floor. 'You talk too much, Cathy,' he admonished. 'Natter, natter, natter—of course I'll take care of Lisa. What else do you expect? We'll return to this house exactly as we leave it, so don't get any ideas to the contrary.'

Lisa looked down at the table, her spirits sinking. Had Catherine got the message? she wondered. To her it was now painfully obvious that Brett had caught the recent gleam in Catherine's eyes, and he had also been well aware of her trend of thought. And by pointing out that they would return to the house exactly as they had left it, he was advising her to forget any matchmaking ideas she might have in mind.

'Come on, let's get cracking.' His tone was abrupt as the command was flung towards Lisa.

Mary was aghast. 'Don't let him boss you in that way!' she advised Lisa. 'Paul never bosses me,' she added proudly.

'He doesn't have to.' Brett's tone was scathing. 'He's got you in the palm of his hand, right where he wants you.'

Catherine gave a light laugh. 'When a man starts bossing a girl it's a sure sign he's determined to dominate her,' she put in smugly. 'If he doesn't try to boss her it means he doesn't care two hoots for her. It's all a matter of male possession.'

Brett's face had become inscrutable. 'Natter, natter, natter!' he snapped at Catherine.

Lisa met his eyes and noted their intangible expression. 'I'll be ready in five minutes,' she told him coolly as she went to her room to collect her shoulderbag, woollen cap and gloves.

A short time later she sat beside him in the silver-grey Holden, and as the car sped westward along a country road bordered by high prickly boxthorn hedgerows she was filled with a quiet contentment. The sun was shining and she was alone with Brett. Previous hurts were wiped from her mind.

At the same time she feared that Catherine's rather frank innuendoes might have put him into a dour and defensive mood for the rest of the day. However, a swift glance at his profile revealed a half-smile hovering about his finely chiselled lips, and she was relieved to see he appeared to have shaken off his former frame of mind that seemed to simmer with irritation.

Actually the sight of the half-smile puzzled her. Could it mean that he too was feeling a surge of inner satisfaction? And could this be because of her own presence? Oh no, Lisa, she told herself firmly. That would be too much to expect. Your own delight in being with him is going to your head, so try and think straight. Get a grip on your senses.

It was these thoughts that made her ask, 'Have you a special reason for making this trip? Is it part of your Search and Rescue work—perhaps checking tracks?'

'No.' He sent her a brief smile. 'Have you forgotten I said I'd take you to Dawson Falls? I like to keep my promises.'

Disappointment drenched her spirits. Of course, she might have guessed it wasn't her company he wanted, it was his own ego that had to be satisfied. 'I quite understand,' she murmured quietly.

The dark eyes sent her a sideways glance. 'You do? What, exactly, do you understand?'

She smiled whimsically. 'That you're doing what you *said* you'd do. You're proving to yourself that you're a man of your word.'

Brett made no attempt to deny the fact, but kept his eyes on the road ahead, until suddenly they were confronted by the stone walls flanking the southern entrance to the Egmont National Park. Beyond it stretched a winding tunnel of towering trees, their roots lost beneath the dense foliage of thick undergrowth, while on the left the ferns clinging to the high bank hung to lap each other like layers of folded wings.

The road became steeper as it followed its ever upward grade, and then, unexpectedly, Brett pulled aside into a wider area that formed a parking bay. 'We can see the falls from here,' he said. 'We're still below three thousand feet and the Tourist Lodge is only a short distance further on.'

They stepped out of the car into the cool air and walked towards a netting and rail fence for Lisa to have her first view of Dawson Falls. A feeling of awe gripped her as she gazed down at the rounded tops of trees growing below, then across the natural amphitheatre of purple-grey rocky cliffs to where the water bubbled and frothed along a narrow stony bed before gushing over the edge.

Brett said, 'It's the Kapuni river. At this place it drops sixty feet, then continues its way to the sea.'

She shuddered. 'I'd hate to fall over the edge!'

He took her arm, holding it in a tight grip as he looked down at her. 'Do you imagine I'd allow you to go near it?'

Her heart leapt at his touch, but she managed to ask calmly, 'Who was Dawson? Why are they called Dawson Falls?'

'Thomas Dawson was a Post Office official who devoted all his spare time to exploring the mountain. He found the falls in 1885 and encouraged the clearing of a camp site nearby.'

'But surely the Maoris knew of the falls before Dawson?'

'Of course. To them the falls were known as Rere-a-Noke, or the Falls of Noke. According to legend he was a man running from the enemy, and it's said he hid from his pursuers by standing behind the falls.'

'Then they shouldn't be known as Dawson Falls,' she protested. 'I much prefer the Maori names.'

'At least we can agree upon that point,' said Brett as, still holding her arm, he led her towards a track that left the road to wind between trees. Again they looked down on the foliage below and then across the amphitheatre to where the bush-covered hills were divided by the river's stony bed.

Lisa pointed upstream. 'Isn't that a bridge crossing the river?'

'Yes—we'll take a walk across it later. In this area there are paths winding all over the place, some of them quite steep. But now we'll go down below to the riverbed.'

She was startled, looking at the drop. 'Down below?' she echoed.

'Don't worry, there are steps.'

He led her farther up the rising road to where a track branched off into the bush. It zigzagged back towards the falls, then descended by steps to the riverbank where the water roared and thundered as it fell into a pool surrounded by large and small boulders, all worn smooth by the passage of time and winter floods. Spray was flung to dampen the myriad ferns growing in the cracks and crevices of the walls, the constant moisture making the smooth boulders slippery.

Brett held Lisa's hand as they wandered about the stony area, and although she did her best to appear nonchalant the pressure from his fingers seemed to send an electric shock into her body. At one point while stepping from boulder to boulder she almost lost her balance and would have fallen but for his quick action in flinging an arm about her waist.

He looked down into her face as she leaned against him, and for one joyous moment she imagined he was about to kiss her. Her breath quickened as his head bent and his lips drew near to her own—but suddenly he released her firmly yet with care. 'Watch your step,' was all he said.

Lisa bit her lip and turned away, fearful that he might read the disappointment in her face.

But he was glancing up at growth on the walls behind them as he said, 'It's time we were making our way up again. You'll find it'll be more difficult than coming down.'

This proved to be a fact—nor had they made much progress before her legs were aching and she was out of breath; but the next instant his arm was again about her waist as he half dragged and half carried her to the top.

'Thank you, Brett,' she gasped as they reached the less strenuous pathway, but already he was striding ahead of her, making his way towards the road.

It didn't take long for him to reach the car, where he stood waiting with the passenger door open for her. She took her seat gratefully, and after a few minutes of negotiating the remaining bends of the upward grade they reached the Tourist Lodge.

Brett parked the car beside several others already in the area. 'You can see we're not the only ones up here,' he said. 'There are always people tramping about the paths during the weekends——' He paused abruptly to look back at one of the cars.

Lisa watched him, a question in her eyes, but he made no comment until they reached the front door of the rambling timber-built Tourist Lodge. He stood still for a moment and glanced about him, but all he said was, 'I'll make arrangements for us to have lunch here, then we'll take a walk up to Wilkie's Pools.'

'Is it far?' she asked, not really caring how great the distance was so long as she was with him.

'About half an hour. The gradient isn't too difficult.'

They turned their backs to the lodge and passed several buildings as they walked towards an opening in the bush which gave access to various routes. Brett indicated the main track leading up to the summit, and several smaller ones branching off to the river.

He described many of the principal landmarks, and as she listened to the sound of his deep voice Lisa realised that this was Brett's kind of country. It was untamed and remote—and a little like Brett himself. And because she loved him she longed to be part of it, to know it as well as he did and to tramp at his side through the bush.

At one clearing she stood still to gaze up at what was known as the Shark's Tooth jutting against the sky from the eastern side of the summit. Woul she ever get near that pointed, sharp-edged rocky formation? It would take real mountain magic to bring about that particular miracle, she thought.

The well-defined path climbed along a narrow ridge, in places skirting steep drops that fell down to the stony bed of the river. Overhead the lichen-covered boughs stretched across to become entwined in a tangled mass of twigs and foliage, and as the higher altitudes were reached the mountain-growing trees became smaller and more scrubby or stunted.

Brett paused at a place where the track branched to

twist down to the riverbed. 'This is where we cross to the other side. Give me your hand.'

Wordlessly she held out her hand. His grip on her own was firm, and for one moment she imagined she saw a message lurking within the depths of his dark eyes. But that was all it was—imagination—because the next instant it had vanished and they were stepping over the water, moving from large smooth boulders to flat slabs of rock.

On the far side the track continued between a growth of tall scrub at river level until it again merged with the river where a further crossing of boulders led to Wilkie's Pools. However, before they could be negotiated a surprise awaited them.

As they moved round a bend in the path they came face to face with two people who walked towards them. Lisa gave a small gasp as she recognised Paul, and she knew that Brett's eyes narrowed as they took in the sight of the girl hanging on his arm.

She was little more than a teenager whose make-up was rather heavy, and whose long blonde hair hung over her shoulders.

# CHAPTER SEVEN

PAUL grinned widely as the distance between them became less. 'Hi there—surprise, surprise!' he exclaimed with forced gaiety, yet without the slightest sign of embarrassment. Nor did he bother to introduce his blonde companion.

Brett remained cool. 'As you say—surprise, surprise. Correct me if I'm mistaken, but didn't you have other arrangements for today? I understood you and Mary were going to Stratford for lunch.'

The blonde giggled, glanced at Paul, then looked at the ground.

Paul was unabashed. 'Oh, *that*. Well, yes, I believe something about lunch at Stratford had been mentioned—but only vaguely, you understand.'

'Mary was anything but vague about it,' snapped Brett.

'Oh well, you know how it is.' Paul sent a glance towards the girl, who simpered at him in a fatuous manner. 'Other things are apt to crop up.'

Brett's mouth thinned to a hard line as he eyed the girl with distaste. 'Obviously.'

Over and over again, Lisa thought to herself. She felt most indignant on Mary's behalf, but was not surprised to discover that Paul had let her down. He hadn't changed at all—not one scrap.

Paul edged further along the path, making it clear he had no wish to remain and prolong the conversation. 'So long, you two—we'll be on our way,' he said breezily as he took the girl's arm and drew her in a leisurely manner towards the crossing stones in the river.

Brett was silent as they walked along the path

towards the slabs of flat rock leading to the pools. His expression had darkened to a scowl and it needed little imagination for Lisa to guess that his mind was filled with Paul and the girl who had clung to his arm in such a possessive manner.

At last, as though making an effort to push the couple from his mind, he said, 'These pools are not what they were when Wilkie found them. Erosion and shifting river stones have wreaked havoc and caused them to lose size and depth.'

Lisa took her cue. 'Who was Wilkie?' she asked, thankful that he was ready to consider another subject. She sat down to rest on a large dry slab and he sat beside her, their closeness seeming to be the most natural thing in the world. She was also conscious of his shoulder within inches of her face, and only with difficulty did she resist the temptation to lean her cheek against it.

'Wilkie?' Brett said absentmindedly. 'He was a farmer who explored whenever the chance presented itself. Most of the tracks were cut by those pioneer climbers, all of them anxious to reach the summit, and each one declaring he had an appointment at the peak.'

He lapsed into silence and Lisa guessed his thoughts were again with Paul and the girl. Confirmation of it came when he turned to her and said with something of an appeal in his voice, 'Tell me, Mary *did* say that Paul was taking her to Stratford—or did I just dream up the whole idea? No, don't bother to answer that question,' he added harshly, 'I know damned well I didn't imagine it.'

'Nor did Paul deny he'd had an arrangement with Mary,' Lisa pointed out.

'Then what the hell was he doing up here with that—that girl?' he exclaimed in exasperated tones.

She sighed. 'I think it's fairly obvious—at least it is to me. He changed his mind because he preferred to do something else. If you don't mind, I'd rather not talk about him.'

He turned to face her. 'Ah, so it got you on the raw, did it? The sight of him with that girl shook you?'

She gave a short laugh. 'Not at all. My days of being shaken by Paul ended a long time ago, as I've already tried to tell you.'

'I still can't help wondering if you've got some sort of feeling for the blighter,' he said moodily.

'Then you can forget it,' she snapped, irritated that he was ruining their pleasant moments together.

'And I'm still wondering if you came here to find him.'

Her patience vanished as she glared at him. 'Can't you understand that if I'd wanted to come chasing after Paul it wouldn't have taken me three years to make a start on the project? Friends in New Plymouth would have soon told me exactly where to find him.'

'Yes, I suppose that's right. Okay, I'll believe you.'

'Thank you. That's good of you.' Her tone was scathing, then she added as a thought struck her, 'You don't appear to know very much about women, Brett.'

He shook his head slowly. 'You're right. They're a pack of sealed mysteries to me. Perhaps I've spent too much time tramping about the mountain.'

'Perhaps you're in love with the mountain instead of with somebody who's real flesh and blood,' she said bitterly, then immediately regretted the words.

Fortunately he ignored them as his thoughts appeared to have switched back to his sister. 'As for Mary, I'll shake the living daylights out of her if she dares to mention Mason's name again!'

'That would be a grave mistake,' Lisa pointed out. 'It would simply throw her straight into his arms. Personally, I think she needs to see Paul in his true colours for herself, just as I had to.'

'Oh? How did it come about?'

She was silent, wishing she could tell him about

Maggie Simpson, but the thought of breaking her word to Paul, despite his faults, went against the grain. Nor did she feel inclined to lay bare the details of her own humiliation. 'I'm afraid I can't tell you anything about it,' she said with cool determination.

'But you will,' Brett declared with some force.

Her brows rose. 'Really? What makes you so sure about that?'

'Because I'll wring it out of you. It's something I want to know, and I intend to find out,' he told her harshly.

She was amazed by the vehemence in his voice. 'I— I can't see that it's any business of yours.'

'Correction: I'm making it my business. Right, shall we go? Have you seen enough of these pools?' He stood up abruptly as though wishing to get right away from the place.

Lisa scrambled to her feet. 'Yes, thank you, I've seen plenty. You sound as though you regret bringing me here. I suppose it's because you saw Paul with his latest interest.' Then, as they made their way back towards the river crossing, she paused to lay a hand on his arm. Looking up into his face, she pleaded, 'Please, Brett, don't let Paul spoil our day. It was so pleasant until you laid eyes on him. After all, it's better for you to know the truth.'

He looked at her intently, but all he said was, 'I'm hungry. Let's go back to the Tourist Lodge for lunch.'

The walk downhill to the Lodge took less time than Lisa had expected, but this was not surprising, because Brett's long legs carried him over the ground so rapidly she had to almost run to keep up with him. He retained a silence which she respected, knowing he was mulling over the problem of his sister and no doubt considering what he should do about it.

On reaching the Lodge she decided to give him a short time to himself, so she made her way to the ladies' where she washed her hands and ran a comb through her hair. When she emerged she noticed an open door leading to an outside veranda, and, wandering through to stand on it, she was confronted by a vast panoramic view of sea and land that disappeared into a haze of distance.

Suddenly she was startled to feel Brett's two hands on her shoulders. He had come unheard through the door behind her, and now the firm pressure of his grip made her throat tighten. She turned her head slowly and was relieved to find that his expression had become more amiable, then a sharp breath escaped her as he bent his head to press his cheek against her own.

'Sunrise is the time to stand on this veranda,' he murmured. 'Golden rays shoot up into the sky and the land looks as if it's in a dreamtime of mists and shadows.'

'You've been here at sunrise?' she whispered, fearful of breaking the spell of his touch.

'Of course.' The admission came quietly.

'But not always alone?' A stab of jealousy caused the words to slip out.

'Definitely not alone.' He gave a short laugh, straightened his back abruptly and removed his hands from her shoulders as he added, 'The bedrooms are just along the corridor. Most people who stay here come out to see the sunrise, and the veranda can be crowded. Shall we go to the dining room?'

Lisa followed him meekly.

Lunch was a delicious meal of smoked eel followed by cold venison and salad. Their table near the window gave an uninterrupted view of the peak with its broken terrain of deep snow-filled gorges, sharp ridges, outcrops of rock and deceptively smooth faces. She gazed towards it longingly, watching the few wispy clouds that gathered to partly hide it from sight before drifting on to leave it clear again.

Brett patted her hand. 'I can see the look in your eyes!' he teased. 'I know the peak's calling to you, but you can't go up there today. It takes at least four and a half hours' climbing from here—not that I'd take you at this time of the year. It's a summertime climb.'

She turned to him eagerly. 'You *would* take me—some day?'

A shutter seemed to drop as his face became inscrutable. 'Perhaps, some day, you might keep an appointment at the peak. Who knows?'

'Who indeed?' She felt vaguely disappointed by his lack of enthusiasm, but listened politely as he spoke of the dangers to be encountered when climbing at certain times of the year. Then, turning again to gaze upward, she was surprised to see that already more clouds had gathered, this time lower and thicker. Nor did they drift away as quickly as before.

Following her gaze, Brett frowned. 'There could be even heavier clouds behind those banks of mist. They'll either go away or come right down.'

'Are you saying you think it might rain?'

'Yes, but I haven't forgotten I promised to take you across the bridge above the falls, so if you've finished your coffee we'd be wise to start moving.'

As they walked past the parking area Lisa noticed that most of the cars had gone, and she then recalled that he had paused to stare back at one of them. And although she was reluctant to bring up the subject of Paul she was unable to resist the question. 'You recognised Paul's car when we first arrived here?'

'Yes. The sight of it puzzled me, especially as I thought it should have been on its way to Stratford. Let's forget about him,' he added harshly.

She was only too glad to do this, and her spirits rose as he led her along paths behind the Tourist Lodge, some of them bordered with ferns and the sharp-edged blades of native grasses. In places she stumbled down leaf-strewn steps that descended to twist and wind beneath the overhanging lichen-draped boughs, and always she thrilled to the touch of his hand beneath her arm, assisting her across places that were slippery and wet from springs.

It was a rambling route, leading down across a small bridge, then up to a track which gave higher lookout places where they paused to gaze at distant wooded humps and hillsides. Brett pointed out several places of interest to climbers, and then they descended to cross the lower and longer bridge near the falls.

Halfway across they paused to lean on the rail and watch the violence of the waters rushing noisily between large rounded river boulders before leaping over the sixty-foot drop. Nor had they been there long before mists and rain descended, to sprinkle their faces and wrap them in a shroud of fog.

Brett said, 'Let's move on. I know where we can shelter beneath a spreading totara tree. Only heavy rain will get through its thick foliage.'

They hastened up the twists and curves until Brett turned along a side track. Taking Lisa's hand, he led her to a secluded area that was surrounded by undergrowth, and where the path ended beside an ancient tree of giant proportions. It was here that he took her in his arms.

The unexpectedness of it took her breath away, nor did she have any wish to fight against the magnetic force that lifted her face up towards his. She closed her eyes as she felt his lips roam over the smoothness of her lids and cheeks before they found her mouth, and as his kiss deepened a surge of intense yearning set her blood on fire.

A deep sigh escaped him as the fingers of one hand unzipped their jackets to remove the restricting thickness of material between them. 'That's better,' he murmured, nuzzling her neck. 'I don't like clothes that keep us apart.'

Lisa became aware of the intense desire that engulfed him, of the primitive male demands of his body calling to her own, and then the firmness of his

hand in the small of her back pressed her even closer
to him, sending her inner flames leaping skywards.

Loving him, she knew that her whole being
responded with a depth of longing that was almost
overwhelming, and she also knew that she ached to
give and give until her strength had vanished. Her
heart thumped, causing her throat to constrict as she
was forced to give an involuntary and uncontrolled
arching towards him.

Clinging to him with wild abandon, she whispered
huskily, 'Brett—oh, Brett—I do——' Then, horrified,
she gulped back the words on the edge of her tongue,
falling silent as she realised she had almost confessed
that she loved him. The knowledge was enough to jolt
her to her senses.

'Yes? You were saying——?' he muttered softly
against her lips, then his hand pressed her head
against the firmness of his chest while his fingers
became entwined in her hair as he awaited her reply.

'Nothing—nothing. I'm just trying to stay sane,' she
gasped. Leaning against him, she could hear the
rhythmic thud-thud of his heart and she knew his
control was nearly at breaking point. Her words grew
muffled as she whispered. 'I—I think we should leave
this place—it's dangerous.'

Brett laughed softly. 'You think a storm might come?'

'A storm has come, and you know it. An emotional
storm.'

'You fear we might make love here, in the rain?'

She remained silent, unable to meet his eyes, yet
knowing she longed to be one with him—anywhere,
even in the rain.

'You're afraid of me, Lisa? You're afraid I'll take
you against your will? Only it wouldn't be against your
will, would it? You want me as much as I want you.'

Her arms clung to him as she buried her face against
his chest, and while she was still unable to look at him
she was also unable to find words of denial.

'I believe you *are* afraid of me.' His deep voice had become little more than a husky whisper.

She nodded. 'Yes, to be honest, I am. You're so—so unpredictable, sometimes a glacier, but at other times, like now, on fire.'

'At the moment a raging furnace,' he admitted, holding her even closer. 'But then you know that, don't you, my lovely Lisa? You know that I want you, that I long to make love with you——'

He kissed her again, and as his lips became possessive his hand slipped beneath her jersey to slide her bra strap aside and cup her bare breast. His fingers fondling her raised nipple drew a further ecstatic response from her until he again held her against his chest, where she waited expectantly for the words that would tell her he loved her, that his desire for her went much, much deeper than mere sex.

Instead he murmured, 'This place could be the Garden of Eden—without the snake, of course. It's a place where lovers steal precious moments.'

'Lovers? You know that *lovers* come here?' A cold chill crept over her as she considered his words. Was he trying to tell her something? And then she almost felt the colour drain from her face as, once again, she was gripped by a spasm of jealousy. 'Is that how you happen to know of this place?' she asked quietly.

He frowned at her. 'What are you trying to say?'

'I mean I'm not the only girl you've brought to this spot.'

Brett laughed softly. 'Silly little goose!'

'Or perhaps, except for the rain, you wouldn't have brought me here at all.' Her tone became accusing as she persisted in torturing herself with the suspicion that this was merely a short interlude, a few moments of amusement while waiting for a shower to pass.

His eyes took on their penetrating glint. 'Something's bugging you, and I'd like to know what it is. Please don't allow it to ruin those moments we've just shared.' His voice had become low. 'You promise?'

Lisa nodded. 'I'll—I'll try.' She swallowed hard as her eyes become moist.

He kissed her again, effectively silencing any further protest until at last he said, 'The rain caused me to remember this place of shelter. However, I think it's eased off now, so perhaps we should leave before it comes on again, and more heavily next time.'

They made their way back to the main track through a veil of mist that cast a ghostly gloom over the dripping branches. The roadway was wet and the car, when they reached it, looked freshly washed. Lisa didn't really want to get into it because she knew it meant the beginning of the end of the day alone with Brett, but as he took his seat behind the wheel he returned to the subject of his sister.

'I've been thinking of Mary,' he admitted casually.

She turned to look at him but said nothing, wondering if, despite his kisses, his sister had been more prominently in his mind than she herself had been. His next words seemed to confirm this suspicion.

'I've been wondering if you'll help her.' He half turned towards her, raising a dark brow.

'Of course. I'll do anything I can—if she'll listen to me.'

'I think she should have a long spell away from home. Does your offer still hold?'

'My offer? Oh, you mean my suggestion that she should come home with me? Naturally, it still stands.'

'Good. When you leave Lynton I'll be grateful if you'll do your best to persuade her to return to Auckland with you. I'm sure it would be the best way to clear her mind.'

Lisa stared straight ahead as the car glided between the bush walls of the winding downhill road. *When you leave Lynton*, he'd said. That meant he had no

thought of her remaining after she had finished
Catherine's book—which in turn meant there had
been neither sincerity nor depth behind his kisses.
They didn't mean anything at all to him.

Cold fingers seemed to be clutching at her heart as
she became conscious of a deepening depression
coupled with the horrible suspicion that she was being
manipulated. Yes, that was the word—*manipulated*.
While holding her in his arms beneath the tree Brett
hadn't been showering her with love and affection at
all—he had been planning and wooing her co-
operation. He had been seeking her aid for Mary. A
surge of indignation shook her, but she told herself to
simmer down and to begin a little clear thinking on
her own accord.

Brett sent her a half smile as the car swung out of
the Egmont National Park. 'You're very thoughtful,'
he remarked. 'What's on your mind? I'm sure it's
constructive.'

'On the contrary, I'm trying to decide exactly what
it is you'd like me to do. I can only presume it's to
hasten the end of *Mountain Memory*, and then for me
to take my departure with Mary.' She found difficulty
in keeping the bitterness from her voice, and waited
anxiously for his denial concerning her departure.

But it did not come. Instead he said, 'I don't see
how you can do more than you're doing at present.
You're already working long hours on it.'

'Nor will Catherine want to see the job rushed,' Lisa
pointed out.

'Perhaps you could persuade her to help with the
typing.'

She shook her head. 'No, I must see to it myself.'
The excuse came readily because in all honesty she
didn't want Catherine to assist with the typing. In fact
she had no wish for any help that would hasten her
departure from Lynton. And then another thought
struck her.

Turning to him, she said urgently, 'Aren't you forgetting Paul's suggestion that he might find a job on the North Shore? If he does, and Mary is there, she'd be right back to square one.' She hesitated, then pointed out, 'If he's in a flat she might even consider moving in with him.'

He gave a harsh laugh. 'Mary? Move in with a man? That'll be the day! She'd never do it.'

Lisa's tone became dry. 'Have you forgotten that the man is Paul? He could be persuasive, if it suited him.'

Brett remained silent, frowning at the road ahead.

Lisa pressed home the vantage. 'Have you also forgotten there's talk of a plan but no mention of marriage? These are modern times, Brett, and Mary is an adult. She'll do exactly as she wishes, especially if the opportunity presents itself. So, if you work it out from *that* angle, the North Shore might not be the best place for her.' She took a quick peep to judge his reaction.

He was noncommittal. 'It's possible you're right. So what do you suggest?'

'I think the matter will solve itself. Sooner or later she'll see the light and will have to face up to the situation.' Just as I'm having to face up to it, she thought dolefully. Mary and I are in the same boat. I also love a man who doesn't love me.

'This is the kind of thing you yourself had to cope with,' Brett said with perception. 'Apparently you ran away.'

'Yes.' Startled, she wondered if he had read her thoughts.

'Do you think Mary should run away?'

'Only if she has something to occupy her mind when she reaches a destination of some sort. I was fortunate in having a father who was very friendly with Gordon Bishop, who happened to have a staff vacancy at that particular time. It gave me my job with the publishing firm.' *And it also brought me to you*, she added silently to herself.

Then they reached home Catherine wasn't even remotely surprised to see them return earlier than expected. 'I told you not to judge the day by the morning,' she reminded Lisa.

'We've more than the weather to discuss,' Brett told her crisply. 'Where's Mary?'

Catherine's brows rose with a hint of surprise. 'Have you forgotten she was going to Stratford? She isn't home yet. The poor girl was so disappointed because she had to go alone. Paul rang to say he'd had to change his plans as something unexpected had cropped up.'

'You can say that again!' Brett snapped. 'The something was a young blonde in the throes of first love and infatuation.'

Catherine's hazel eyes widened as she looked at him incredulously. 'Are you saying he let Mary down for somebody else?'

'That's exactly what I'm saying, and I doubt that it's the first time.' He went on to tell her about the meeting with Paul near Wilkie's Pools.

Catherine's mouth tightened as she listened, then she turned to Lisa. 'You've tried to warn us, but we haven't really listened——'

Brett cut in, 'The point is that something has to be done about the situation. I might add, Catherine, that it was your matchmaking activities that got Mary into it, so perhaps you can come up with a suggestion that'll get her out of it.'

'I was only trying to do my best for her,' Catherine protested. She fell silent, thinking deeply, then came to a decision as she said, 'I'll put a call through to New Plymouth. Laura and the two girls might be able to help. Perhaps Mary could visit them for a while. It'd be a nice change for her—if she'll go.'

'Explain the situation fully so that they won't allow

her to sit in a corner like a moping mouse,' Brett advised.

Catherine left the room, her attitude full of purpose.

'Who are Laura and the girls?' Lisa felt compelled to ask.

'Laura is my aunt,' he explained. 'She was my mother's younger sister. Her two daughters, Susan and Sally, are my cousins. When Laura's husband died she knew she had to be kept occupied, so she and the girls pooled their resources to build a block of motels on the front lawn of their home. It's on the sea-front, and because it's near town they're kept very busy.'

*A motel on the sea-front.* Lisa grew thoughtful as she remembered Paul's words concerning Maggie Simpson. She's working at a waterfront motel, he'd said. Could it be the same one? Her eyes narrowed as she tried to recall suitable sites for motels along the New Plymouth sea-front, but there were very few.

At last she said, 'Do you really believe Mary will go to them?'

'It's possible, by the time I've finished talking to her. Will you add your persuasion?'

Lisa shook her head. 'Definitely not. She'd suspect my motives for wishing her to be away from this place. I'm sure she still believes I came here to find Paul.'

'I noticed you remained very calm when he appeared with that girl. Or were you concealing an inner fury?'

'I'll admit I was angry, but it was purely on Mary's behalf. Can't you believe me?' She looked at him pleadingly.

'I'm wrestling with it.' There was a mocking glint in his eyes.

'In any case, you yourself took the meeting very calmly,' Lisa added.

'Did you expect me to punch him on the nose? I'll admit it gave me a shock, and my instinct was to knock his block off until one salient fact leapt into my mind.'

Lisa looked at him stonily. 'A fact that exonerates Paul, no doubt? You men always stick together.'

'That's possible. Nevertheless it occurred to me that I'm unaware of any definite commitment between Paul and Mary. As far as I know he's a free man, so he doesn't have to explain himself to her or to anyone else. Perhaps the situation between them is something she's built up in her own mind——'

His explanation was cut short as Catherine returned to the room. 'It couldn't be better,' she declared happily. 'Laura hasn't been well and has had quite a spell in bed.'

Brett's brows shot up. 'That's a good thing?'

'Of course. Don't you see? Susan and Sally need extra help. They've still got that girl Maggie who comes in to vacuum and clean the bedrooms, but Mary would be a godsend and they'd be delighted to see her arrive.'

Lisa listened with interest. So it *was* the same motel. She longed to tell them that Mary would soon learn all about Paul, but decided to remain silent.

Brett said, 'Laura's illness will enable you to tell Mary she's duty bound to assist her aunt and cousins.'

'Exactly. And there's something else. They've had the two back bedrooms of their own house knocked into one large room where they hold parties and dances. This means that young people staying in the motel can have their fun and loud music without disturbing other guests. Susan said it's being used every night. Don't you see? It means that Mary will meet more people.'

'And about time too,' Brett rasped.

'I've arranged for Susan to ring her later and ask if she'll go to New Plymouth and give them a hand. I thought it the best way.'

Brett sent her an approving glance. 'Bless you, Cathy! When it comes to manipulation you're out on your own—a real expert!'

When Mary arrived home an hour later she was wearing an air of depression, and although she tried to escape to her bedroom she was waylaid by Brett, who drew her into the living room.

Watching her narrowly, he said, 'Did you have a good day? Paul picked you up on time, I presume?' The question came smoothly.

Her eyes moistened as she shook her head. 'No, I—I had to go alone. He—he rang to say he couldn't make it. Apparently something cropped up.'

'I'll say it did!' Brett snapped. 'Come into the library, I want to talk to you. I'll tell you exactly what cropped up. It's got long blonde hair draped round its shoulders——'

Later, when they emerged from the library, Mary's face was tear-stained. She disappeared into her bedroom, refusing to join them for evening meal, but when the phone in the hall rang she rushed to pick up the receiver. A few minutes later she appeared at the dining room door, her eyes still wide from the surprise of the phone call.

'Was that Paul?' Catherine asked with casual innocence.

'No, it was Susan ringing from New Plymouth. She says Aunt Laura's sick and they could do with a little extra help. They're wondering if I'll give them a hand.'

'Of course you must go at once,' said Catherine as if it was already settled. 'Take my large suitcase from the boxroom. You might stay longer than you expect.'

'Susan said to be sure and bring a couple of party dresses, and something about having their own dance floor——'

'Really? That's nice,' Catherine murmured.

Mary looked at her suspiciously. 'You don't sound a bit surprised that they have their own dance floor? Did you *know*?'

'It's not surprising at all,' Brett cut in sharply.

'They're enterprising girls who don't waste their time mooning over idiots who consider themselves to be God's gift to women.'

Mary sent him a baleful glare, then disappeared towards the boxroom, which was next to the laundry.

Next morning she left immediately after breakfast.

They waved goodbye, and as the small car disappeared along the drive Catherine heaved a sigh of relief. 'Thank goodness that plan worked well,' she said.

'A most satisfactory effort on your part, Cathy dear,' Brett put in dryly. 'I congratulate you. Well now, what are your plans for today?'

'I'll be busy with my usual Sunday letter-writing stint. I've thought of several people who could help me contact the descendants of further pioneer women. Why do you ask?'

'I wondered if you'd like to come with us,' he said casually.

'Oh? You're taking Lisa out somewhere?' Catherine looked surprised but sounded pleased.

'Yes. We're going along the coast road west of the mountain to see a stock-breeder who has a new line of pedigree Jersey bulls.'

Catherine's brows rose with a hint of disapproval. 'You're taking Lisa to look at *bulls*? Isn't that rather—er—indelicate?'

Brett laughed. 'We're out of the Victorian era now, Cathy, even if your head's full of what your pioneer women would see fit to do. However, Lisa can wait in the car while I examine this animal—but a new bull is something I must have. Old George will be coming back on his own progeny if I don't get him off the place.'

'I understand,' Catherine said hastily. Then, to Lisa, 'You'll enjoy seeing the coast road—it's rather primitive.'

Lisa's surprise was still apparent as she said. 'This is the first I've heard of the trip. I had intended getting on with the job in the library.'

Brett smiled easily. 'A little tiger for work, aren't

you? You're forgetting I said you wouldn't be working on Sundays.'

'You're being very high-handed,' she retorted with a touch of indignation. 'How come you're examining a bull on Sunday?'

'Because it suits me to do so,' he declared loftily. 'However, if you're so madly keen on work you can bring something to do while I look at the bull.'

'Very well, I'll do that,' she replied quietly, at the same time secretly scorning herself for not having the willpower to refuse to accompany him. She knew she didn't have to go with him, yet it seemed as though an unseen electrical force pulled her towards him. I suppose it's because I love him, she thought helplessly, then, fearful that it might be revealed in her face, she lowered her head and went to the library where she put together a neat pack of scribbling paper and manuscript pages.

They had lunch early and it was still only one o'clock when the plates were stacked into the dishwasher. Brett drove the Holden to the back door, and as Lisa took her seat beside him he leaned over to make sure her seat-belt was correctly adjusted.

She revelled in his attention, a small sigh of contentment escaping her, and although she was unaware of it a faint smile played about her lips.

'You're comfortable?' he asked solicitously.

Lisa nodded. 'Perfectly, thank you.' She breathed deeply, taking in the pleasant odour of his aftershave.

'The seat-belt isn't too tight?'

She shook her head. 'No, it's fine.'

Nevertheless he ran his hand beneath its length to judge the tension, and in doing so his fingers lingered momentarily on her breast.

'You're resigned to coming out with me?' he teased.

'Quite resigned.' She smiled happily and her eyes shone. She was going out with Brett, so, at the moment, what more could she wish for?

# CHAPTER EIGHT

BRETT was about to turn the ignition key when Catherine called to him from the back door. 'Wait, you'd better take this—you might like to have a picnic at some place.' She carried a basket towards the car and put it on the back seat. It contained a thermos of tea, cups and a cookie jar.

'Thank you, Cathy—that's thoughtful of you,' said Brett.

She regarded them both with a look of pleased speculation. 'You're sure to want a hot drink. You might even find a nice cosy place to park—somewhere secluded.'

'Thank you—you're very kind,' said Lisa. She met the hazel eyes and was suddenly startled by the expression they held. It was almost as though Catherine was trying to send her a secret message.

'Good luck—have a happy—a *very* happy afternoon!' The older woman's smile was almost roguish.

Lisa was puzzled. There seemed to be a depth of meaning behind the words, and as she pondered them a slight flush rose to her cheeks. *Good luck?* What on earth did Catherine mean by that remark? Her colour deepened as she wondered if Catherine suspected her feelings towards Brett. Was it her way of saying she approved? And—horror of horrors—had Brett caught any hint, or noticed the expression in his stepmother's eyes? She peeped at him as the car swung on to the road, but his face betrayed nothing.

They drove in silence while her mind continued to question Catherine's wish for good luck, and the more she thought about it the more embarrassed she became. *Of course* Catherine had guessed she was in love with Brett, and while she'd tried to keep it from being written all over her face Catherine's shrewd eyes and womanly instinct had glimpsed the truth.

And in that moment Lisa realised she had been deliberately brought to Lynton to be laid across Brett's path. She, too, had been manipulated into becoming part of one of Catherine's matchmaking schemes.

Nevertheless she felt compelled to ask, 'What did Catherine mean by—by good luck?'

Brett shrugged. 'Who knows? Cathy's good at making enigmatic remarks. In this case she was probably wishing me luck in the purchase of a good bull. Sometimes a bull can be disappointing.'

'Oh, I see.' Lisa stared straight ahead. She was not at all convinced that this was what Catherine had meant.

The road headed westward towards the southern end of Cape Egmont passing through several small settlements as it skirted the lower slopes of the mountain. And as the car glided along the tarsealed surface Brett chatted amicably, pointing out places of interest along the route.

Lisa listened in silence, making little or no comment until she was startled by an abrupt question.

'Am I boring you?'

'No, of course not. I'm interested to see the places mentioned in Catherine's manuscript.'

He thought for a moment, then asked, 'Do you intend to stay and help her with the book about the early women?'

The suggestion surprised her. 'Oh no, I don't think Catherine expects me to do that. After all, it's *her* book—and in any case Mr Bishop expects me to be back in the office as soon as possible.'

She peeped at him, longing to hear him utter words giving reasons why she should prolong her stay, but they did not come.

Frowning at the road ahead, he said, 'I can't see that
*Mountain Memory* is Catherine's book any longer, and
I'm beginning to suspect she now looks upon it as
being your book.'

'That's ridiculous,' she protested. 'I've merely
reorganised the material she spent years in gathering.
It needed editing, and that's all I'm doing. Perhaps
you could say I'm a little like a ghost writer,' she
smiled.

His dark eyes flashed a sweeping glance over her
slim form. 'A more attractive ghost I've yet to meet,'
he commented dryly.

The unexpectedness of the compliment sent her
spirits soaring upward, and a wave of quiet contentment caused her to relax. A warm companionship
seemed to spring up between them, and as they drove
in silence the car radio offered soft music. A soothing
male voice sang about *Memories*—and although their
hours together had only begun, instinct told Lisa that
the afternoon would be unforgettable.

At last she glanced at him, a slight smile playing
about her soft lips. Did he also feel relaxed and
contented? Was it possible she was filling his thoughts
even as he filled hers? 'You're very quiet,' she
remarked.

'Am I? Actually my thoughts have been with
Dreaming Sam.'

She felt nettled. 'Dreaming Sam? Who on earth is
he?'

'He's the bull I'm about to purchase—providing he
appears to be a satisfactory animal.'

'Oh.' Lisa felt deflated as she realised the bull had
held priority over herself in his thoughts.

'George Jones assures me he comes from an
excellent line. Jones is the breeder, you understand,'
added Brett as he reduce speed to turn along a side
ride.

A short time later the car turned into a drive that led

towards a white timber-built homestead. Brett drove into a large yard at the rear, and as he did so a short sturdily-built man came through the back door of the house.

Lisa was introduced briefly to George Jones, who wasted no time in handing a stud book to Brett. The two men left the car and she sat watching as they moved through a gate and began to cross a field towards a set of railed yards where a large animal stood waiting. That must be Dreaming Sam, she thought.

Her eyes rested on Brett's athletic form striding across the grass, and she noticed that the stock-breeder's short legs had to move swiftly to keep up with him. Then, dragging her mind away from Brett, she reached over to the back seat for the work she had brought with her.

Fifteen minutes later she raised her eyes from the papers on her knee and was in time to see the men returning through the gate. The look of satisfaction on George Jones' face seemed to indicate that he had made a sale, and as they crossed the yard towards the house she saw Brett take his cheque book from his inner breast pocket. However, another ten minutes passed before he took his seat behind the wheel.

She replaced her work on the back seat. 'You've bought him?' she asked as he turned on the ignition.

'Yes. He's a well-grown two-year-old—a perfectly balanced bull, with all his points in good proportion.

'What do you look for?' She found herself genuinely interested.

'A nice straight back, good deep shoulders and a head that's neither too large nor too small. And there's also his breeding in the stud book to be considered. This fellow's been bred in the purple. I presume you know what that means?'

She shook her head. 'Not really.'

'It means the top line of today's breeding. Dreaming

Sam was sired by Sleepy Samson who'd been sired by Dozy Joe—whose dam had been the famous Josephine.'

'I'm glad the females get a little recognition,' she smiled.

'You can bet they do! They're very important and have to be excellent producers of milk that's high in quality and quantity. Dairy cows are not allowed to luxuriate on the best pastures for no reason at all. They have to earn the privilege of delivering the goods to go into the milk tanker.'

Lisa looked at the herds grazing in the fields. 'They look so peaceful and contented,' she remarked.

'You're sure you're not bored with all this talk about cows and bulls? I dare say you'll be glad to leave it all behind when you return to Auckland.'

His words were like a douche of cold water, but she managed to say quietly, 'I'm not bored, nor am I aching to return to Auckland.'

Brett glanced at the papers on the back seat. 'I see you did some work while you waited. How is it all progressing?'

'Aren't you really asking when do I think I'll be finished and on my way?'

'Not at all—but what stage have you reached?' His voice held mild curiosity.

'I'm working on Catherine's material about this western side of the mountain, so I'm interested to see the formation of the land and the way the ridges and valleys sweep down to the sea. Thank you for bringing me.'

'It's a pleasure.' He reached over and patted her hand, and the action coupled with the smile he gave her made her breath quicken. He added, 'Perhaps I should show you the actual coastline. It's not too far away.'

He drove in silence for several minutes, then turned along a side road which eventually ended at a wide grassy plateau above the sea. To the left and right stretched long lines of sheer dark-faced cliffs that dropped down to a bleak and lonely shore where waves pounded against ominous rocks embedded in black sand.

They left the car and he guided her to where a nearby break in the cliffs formed a valley. A rough track descending along one side enabled them to make their way down to the sands, where they walked for a distance between large rocks and rounded stones.

The breeze whipped colour into Lisa's cheeks and blew her hair into a dark auburn halo through which the afternoon sun shot glints of red. Yet despite the sun's warmth she shuddered. 'It all looks so forbidding—a nightmare coast!'

As the wind became stronger Brett took her arm and drew her towards the shelter of a sandbank at the foot of the cliffs. It protected them from the gusts, and as they sat down beside it he pointed towards the distant bare faces. 'The Taranaki coast is noted for its perpendicular shoreline,' he told her. 'Some of the cliffs have caves beneath them.'

'But the sand is so black,' she complained, allowing a handful to trickle through her fingers. 'I like sand to be golden—it's cleaner, and somehow so much more romantic.'

He stared out to sea. 'Romantic? I know very little about romance. As for the black sand, one becomes accustomed to it, especially when its value is realised,' he added dryly. 'It's used for the production of steel and is mined for export, mainly to Japan. Doesn't Catherine's book mention it?'

'No. Black sand into steel is something the early settlers failed to dream about.'

He gave a small sound of impatience, at the same time lying back and stretching his length against the lower contour of the sandbank. 'Forget the early settlers—they've gone. Switch your mind to the present—it's ours.' The words came abruptly. It was a command, and he turned to watch its effect on her.

'You're right,' she agreed. 'My mind has become so entangled I don't know whether I'm in today or yesterday.'

'Then lie beside me and relax.' It was a further command, and his hand came up to draw her down to the sand.

Lisa lay back obediently, listening to the roar of the surf and gazing at clouds that scudded across the sky. At the same time she made an effort to stem her own inner turmoil which had been stirred by the realisation that she was actually lying beside him on the beach. It seemed incredible. Take it calmly, Lisa, she warned herself silently. Don't make a fool of yourself.

They lay in silence for several minutes until Brett made a sudden move to raise himself on one elbow to stare at her. 'There now, isn't that more comfortable?'

She nodded without meeting his eyes, although she knew they raked her face, examining every feature as they glided from her brow to her mouth, then from her throat to the rounded rise of her breasts.

'You're very beautiful, Lisa,' he said at last.

She accepted the compliment gracefully. 'Thank you. I never trouble to think about it.' His words had fired an inward glow.

'I suppose Paul has mentioned the fact on numerous occasions?'

She gave a slight shrug. 'It's possible. I really can't remember. Do we have to talk about him?'

'Really finished with him, are you?'

A sigh of exasperation escaped her. 'How many times do I have to tell you?' Frustrated, she closed her eyes and turned her face away from him.

'Okay, okay, I'd just like to be assured of the fact.'

She felt his fingers stroking the hair at her temples. They traced the fine arches of her brows before wandering to follow the contour of her cheeks, then moving to rest near her lips.

'Look at me, Lisa,' he persuaded gently.

She was afraid to, fearing that her love for him would blaze from her eyes and speak for itself.

The firm strength of his hand forced her face towards him. 'Look at me, Lisa,' he repeated quietly.

Her lids fluttered open and as her confused gaze met the intensity of his eyes his arms gathered her body to him, pressing and moulding her against his own. His head bent slowly until their lips met, softly at first and then with increasing passion.

A surge of happiness engulfed her, sending tingles of joy racing through her entire being. Did Brett love her? Surely he couldn't possibly hold her like this, kiss her like this, unless he loved her. It remained only for him to tell her, to ask her to marry him——

His hand unzipped her jacket and she made no protest as it found its way beneath her jersey to cup her breast. His thumb stroked her raised nipple gently, sending spasms of primitive desire shooting through her veins, twitching at nerves that were as taut as violin strings.

'I want you, Lisa,' he murmured huskily against her lips. 'You know I want you.'

She nodded wordlessly, her heart too full for speech. There was no need to be told of his burning male longing that cried out to reach and mingle with her own yearning. And she knew that at any moment now he would tell her loved her.

'I know you want me, Lisa. You're a woman, with a woman's needs. I know you're on fire——' His lips found their way to her breast, causing her to give a small strangled cry as she felt all control melting like mist in the sun. But still he hadn't said he loved her— the all-important words hadn't been uttered.

'Tell me you want us to make love——' His voice was a deep husky murmur, vibrant with emotion.

Lisa stirred in his arms. 'You mean here, on the sand?'

'The beach is isolated. What better place than beneath the sky, the only sound being the breaking of waves and the cry of a gull?' His hand slipped beneath the belt of her track-suit, feeling the smoothness of her hips.

The action caused cool reasoning to seep into her brain as she stared at a seagull flying overhead. Wasn't he going to tell her he loved her? Apparently the words were not in his mind at all. These moments so precious to herself were merely an incident that would satisfy his male sexual needs. They were, in fact, like that bird with its white wings outspread against the blue sky—here only briefly and then gone without a trace to show they had ever existed.

Suddenly she was thankful that he hadn't said he loved her because she knew that if he had uttered the words she would have given herself to him. Her longing had been so intense there would have been no hesitation. But obviously he did not love her and could see no reason to lie about it, and for this much she was grateful.

In some way Brett sensed her sudden coolness. He removed his hand from her belt, turned on to his back and lay still for several moments before he said, 'What's the matter, Lisa?'

'Nothing.' Her voice came as a muffled whisper.

'You can't fool me. Something tells me you've gone cold. Why?' He leaned over and stared into her face.

She made an attempt to sound normal. 'Actually, I *am* feeling a little cold. Perhaps it's the breeze or the coolness of the sand.'

'It's more than that. Something also tells me you don't want us to make love. Why, Lisa? Tell me why?' His voice was urgent.

'You—you wouldn't understand.' She turned her face away.

'Try me and see.' The words came harshly.

She sat up abruptly, searching for words and fighting her tears. 'Because—because—I think I'd rather have a cup of tea.'

'*Cup of tea?* Hell's bells, you can't mean it!'

'Yes, I can—and I *do*. Catherine put it in the car. It's on the back seat waiting for us. It'd be dreadful to take it home untouched after her trouble preparing it for us——'

She sprang to her feet and ran as swiftly as she could, making her way over the stones and dodging between the rocks. Tears blurred her vision and stung coldly on her cheeks, but still she raced along, hardly pausing for breath when she came to the cliffside track, and panting laboriously as she made her way up it.

A hasty glance over her shoulder showed that Brett followed slowly, and by the time he had reached the car she had dabbed at her eyes, powdered her nose and had better control over her emotions.

The sipped their tea in silence until Brett said coldly, 'Were you trying to make a fool of me, Lisa?'

The suggestion amazed her. 'Me? Make a fool of you? I don't know what you mean.'

'I think you do. You called to me, then slammed the door in my face.'

Her jaw dropped. 'I—called to *you*? Well, I like that!' she flared indignantly. 'As I see it, it was the other way round. It was *you* who led *me* to that isolated place. It was *you* who pulled *me* down on to the sands—your only intention being to use me to satisfy yourself. Then let me tell you this, Brett Arlington, I don't intend to be used in that way!' Her voice rang with accusation as she almost choked on the last words.

'You're quite wrong, Lisa,' he said quietly.

'Oh? In what way am I wrong?' She turned towards him hopefully. Was he about to tell her he'd wanted

her because he loved her, that he was not using her to
satisfy his own sexual needs?

But he said nothing, finishing his tea in glum silence
as he stared through the front windscreen towards the
surf that pounded over the black sands.

Following his gaze, Lisa knew that the scene
reflected her own inner turmoil and the darkness of
her depression. And as her eyes moved towards the
heavy clouds gathering on the western horizon she
wondered if there could be worse to come.

A short time later, with the thermos and cups
packed into the basket, Brett snapped abruptly, 'Well,
I presume that's that, Lisa. You have no need to fear
for any further cause for complaint from me. In future
I'll control my imagination. When I see that come-
hither look in your eyes I'll know it's pure fancy on
my part. I'll understand it doesn't mean a thing.' He
switched on the motor and the engine roared as he
turned the car and headed for home.

Lisa remained silent during the journey, her heart
heavy, and when they reached Lynton she was aware
that Catherine watched them closely. The sharp hazel
eyes moved from Brett to herself until at last the
question came.

'Well now, tell me everything. How did it go?'
Catherine asked with a hint of bright expectation.

'How did what go, Cathy?' drawled Brett.

Lisa met the glint in the dark eyes. It was almost as
though he was asking Catherine whether she meant
the purchase of Dreaming Sam, or his moments on the
beach with herself.

'The bull, of course,' Catherine pursued. 'I presume
you bought the animal?'

'Yes. He'll take up residence as soon as I can
arrange with the transport firm to bring him here.' His
eyes were still on Lisa, an enigmatic expression on his
handsome face.

Lisa was still clutching the bundle of work she had

brought in from the car. 'I'll return these papers to the library,' she said hastily as she left the room to escape the accusation that had crept into his gaze.

The library with its book-lined walls felt like a haven of refuge, and instead of leaving it immediately she settled down to work with an urgency that helped to brush her emotional problems into the background. Nor did she leave it before Catherine called her for the evening meal, her excuse being that she wanted to make up for lost time. However, there were moments when her concentration slipped— moments when her mind flicked back to the beach, and although she longed for Brett to come into the library his absence made it clear he had no wish to do so.

During the following week her determination to keep her thoughts under control never wavered, although there were moments when difficulties raised their heads. There were times when she heard Brett's footsteps in the hall. Her heart quickened as she paused and waited for him to enter the room, but this never happened. His steps passed on and she was then conscious of deep disappointment. As he had indicated, he was finished with her.

And then an incident occurred which really upset her. It happened late on Wednesday afternoon when Catherine had driven to Eltham for mid-week stores, and after Gwen Yates had left for home. The house was silent until Lisa heard the steps in the hall.

Pen poised, her pulses racing, she heard them stop outside the library, but it wasn't Brett who pushed the door further open—it was Paul. In his arms he carried a large bouquet of flowers—carnations mixed with gladioli in shades of pinks, yellows and orange. The gold ribbons, cellophane and green waxed paper indicated a florist's arrangement, and as he laid it on the table she could only gape at it in silence.

At last she found her tongue and raised questioning

eyes to his face. 'These are for Mary? A peace-offering, no doubt.'

He made no denial but asked, 'Where is she?'

'Staying with relatives. That's all I can tell you.'

'I suppose Brett told her he saw me last Saturday. He couldn't get to her quickly enough, I'll bet!' His tone held a sneer.

'Naturally she was told why you'd let her down,' Lisa told him evenly. 'Brett gave her a full description of the bundle of charms that had happened to crop up.'

'Huh, I'll bet he did!' Paul's mouth twisted.

Lisa glanced at the bouquet lying on the table. 'Does your blonde friend know you've brought these flowers to Mary?'

He shrugged the suggestion away. 'Of course not. In any case she's gone home to Inglewood. She was only here for the weekend.'

'But no doubt she'll be back?'

Paul looked amused. 'It's possible. She's the niece of my share-milker. She's just left school and everything's new to her.'

'Ah, a fresh bloom to be plucked from the field, crumpled and then tossed aside,' accused Lisa.

'Maybe. A bit cloying, though. Nor am I keen on clinging vines. But never mind about her—I want to know about Mary. When did she leave?'

'As soon as she was able to see the light.'

'I can at least apologise to her. What's the address of these relatives?'

'I've no idea. You'd have to get it from Catherine or Brett—that's if they'll give it to you, of course.'

Brett's voice spoke from the doorway. 'Get what from Catherine or Brett?' Ignoring Paul, he strode into the room and stood glaring at the flowers which were making a colourful splash on the table.

'He wants Mary's address,' Lisa explained.

'He's got a damned nerve!' snapped Brett. 'I doubt that she'd want to see him.'

'That's for her to decide,' Lisa pointed out.

'If she's got any sense she'll tell him to go hopping sideways,' snarled Brett, still scowling at the flowers.

Paul made a sound of protest. 'I say, you two, I'm still here you know!' He became affable, ignoring Brett's belligerent attitude by changing the subject and moving towards the table to examine the neat piles of paper. 'By Jove, Lisa, you've sure been getting on with the job!'

'Yes. I'll begin typing next week, and that will be the first step towards the end.'

'You'll be going back to Auckland?' Paul asked casually.

'Of course—where else would I go?' She glanced at Brett. Had he caught the quaver in her voice she'd been unable to control?

Paul said, 'Well, I'll see you there. You'll recall I said I'd thought of applying for a job on the North Shore. I've had an answer from an accountant who used to work in New Plymouth with my father, and I'm taking a trip to see him next week. There's no doubt about it—it's not what you know but who you know.' His light laugh of pleased satisfaction indicated that, for him, getting a job would be the easiest thing in the world.

Lisa looked at him in silence, her spirits plummeting to zero. On the North Shore Paul would be more than capable of making a real nuisance of himself, and this fact seemed to be confirmed as he made his way to the door.

'Cheerio for now,' he grinned. 'I'll call and see you at the office—we'll go down to the beach at Takapuna——'

'Wait!' Brett's voice cut the air like sleet. 'You're forgetting your flowers. You'd better take them, as Mary's not here.'

Paul's grin became even wider. 'Oh, they're not for Mary. I knew she wasn't here because Gwen Yates told my share-milker's wife she'd gone to New Plymouth. They're for Lisa, of course. Who else?' Another laugh and he had gone.

In the silence that followed his exit Lisa felt herself go cold with anger. She spun round to face Brett. 'He's lying, of course. I hope you realise he's lying. They were for Mary.'

His voice became hard. 'Don't try to dodge the issue, Lisa. They were *not* for Mary and you know it. Didn't he admit he knew she'd gone to New Plymouth?'

She shook her head helplessly. 'Well, I'm not accepting them.'

'Okay, if you don't want them I'll be only too glad to toss them out on to the rubbish heap.'

Catherine's voice came to them. 'Toss what on the rubbish heap?' She stood in the doorway, having returned from Eltham earlier than expected, and her eyes were riveted on the flowers as she moved towards the table for a closer examination. 'They're beautiful!' she exclaimed. 'I don't know when I've seen such long-stemmed carnations. And these lovely gladioli——'

'Paul brought them for Lisa,' Brett gritted angrily. 'He knew Mary wasn't here, so they must be for Lisa.'

His eyes held a strange glitter that puzzled Lisa. Surely he couldn't be jealous because Paul had brought flowers for her? Her heart lifted at the thought, then sank as she realised that yes, Paul *had* brought them for her.

Catherine said briskly, 'Well, whoever they're for, they're certainly not going out on to the rubbish heap. I'll take care of them.' She swept the flowers into her arms and carried them away to the kitchen.

The momentary silence that followed her exit was broken by Brett. 'She's taking it very calmly,' he said with a hint of surprise in his voice.

Lisa's brows rose. 'Calmly? What do you mean?'

'To be honest, I expected her to become all agitato. Annoyed, in other words.'

'I'm afraid I don't understand. Why should she be annoyed?'

'Because Paul bringing flowers for you is not in accordance with her own plans,' he explained patiently.

'Plans? I don't know what you're talking about.' Her eyes were wide, the shadowed room causing them to take on their ocean-depths blue.

'I think you understand very well. You're not so dumb you haven't guessed she has plans—for us.'

Lisa found herself unable to look at him, and to hide her acute embarrassment she moved to the window where she stared out at the gathering gloom. 'Are you accusing her of—matchmaking?' she asked at last.

'Of course. It's been obvious to me for some time.'

She swung round to face him. 'Really? Why this sudden change? If I remember correctly you were positive I'd come here with the express purpose of finding Paul. Are you saying you've changed your mind on that point?'

'Have you never heard the old Spanish proverb—a wise man changes his mind, but a fool, never?'

'That's not answering my question.'

'So what if I have changed my mind? I'll admit I was mistaken. At first the conviction that you'd come searching for Paul was strong enough to put me off the scent. It clouded my vision to the extent of blinding me to Catherine's tactics—until Gordon Bishop proved otherwise.'

'Gordon Bishop?' Lisa was surprised. 'When did he do that?'

'When I spoke to him on the phone. He assured me that Catherine was determined to have the manuscript edited under her supervision at Lynton.'

'But there's been so very little supervision,' she pointed out.

'Exactly.' Brett's mouth took on a hard line. 'And that makes it clear you were manipulated into coming here to be laid across my track. Can't you see that?'

This was not something Lisa cared to admit, so she forced herself to give a light laugh. 'Don't worry, I'll get off your track as soon as possible,' she promised, 'especially when I recall your words up on the mountain.'

He frowned. 'My words? What did I say?'

She quoted him. 'You said that any girl brought into your house with a view to matrimony would get short shrift. She'd be tossed out on her neck and right smartly at that. Okay, message received.' She turned away from him and again stared through the window, this time unseeingly.

# CHAPTER NINE

BRETT crossed the room to stand beside her. His face was earnest, his mouth set into a firm line. 'Please believe me, those words spoken on the mountain were not meant to give offence. At that stage I hadn't woken up to Catherine's little game. I hadn't realised she'd brought you here with more than the editing job in mind.'

'Please don't let the situation concern you,' Lisa lashed at him haughtily, her chin in the air. 'I doubt that I'd marry you if you were the last man on earth!' It was a blatant lie, but pride forced the words from her lips.

'I'll marry a girl when I know I can't live without her,' he gritted in even tones.

'That's if she'll accept you,' she snapped back.

'True. Obviously it's useless trying my luck with *you*,' he drawled mockingly.

'Quite,' she retorted, her heart twisting. 'But perhaps you could enlighten me on one point. Suppose Paul *did* bring me flowers, why should you be so angry about it?'

'Who says I'm angry?' he demanded quietly.

'You're not? You could have fooled me! In that case, do you mind if I get on with my job?' She turned to the table and sat down at the manuscript. 'I'd like to get it finished as soon as possible.'

'So you can hurry home to the beach on the North Shore. I understand perfectly,' he snapped, then strode from the room.

For several moments Lisa saw the papers on the table through a blue of tears, controlled only by an effort. Concentration became difficult, and at times she paused as Brett's face rose before her vision and snippets of their conversation echoed in her ears.

His attitude puzzled her. She knew she had not been mistaken, and that he *had* been annoyed because Paul had brought her flowers. Nor had his anger been on Mary's behalf—so why should he be upset to this extent?

Nor was the incident of the flowers forgotten as quickly as Lisa could have wished. Catherine was delighted with them and soon had them artistically arranged in suitable containers which she placed in the lounge and hall, where they stood as colourful reminders of Paul Mason.

'They're so beautiful,' she said to Lisa during the evening meal. 'You should have a vase in the library.'

'No, thank you.' Lisa's tone was firm. 'I'd prefer to have a small bowl of blue and yellow violas from the garden.'

Brett's amused glance indicated that he didn't believe her. 'Be honest,' he taunted. 'Beneath it all you're glowing with quiet satisfaction. You know perfectly well that a rugby, racing and beer type of man is not one to carry flowers. It was probably an effort for Paul to walk into the florist shop. It proves you must mean something very important to him.'

'Brett's right,' Catherine said thoughtfully. 'New Zealand men are not noted for their flower-buying activities. They're not like the Continentals, to whom it's second nature. Nor has Paul ever brought flowers for Mary——'

Lisa snatched at the opportunity to change the subject. 'Have you heard from Mary?' she asked.

Catherine shook her head. 'She hasn't even phoned. I'll admit I'd like to be sure she's settling down fairly happily in New Plymouth, but if I ring her it might make her homesick.'

'Perhaps you're wise to leave well alone,' Brett agreed.

However, Mary's state of mind was revealed to them the following Monday. They were sitting at lunch when she walked into the room—a smiling Mary who appeared to be entirely different from the unhappy girl who had driven from the house almost a fortnight previously.

Catherine's eyes narrowed as she observed her. 'You've come home to stay?'

'No. Only to collect some clothes,' Mary told her brightly. 'Don't get up—I can help myself to some of that soup.'

Brett waited for her to be seated at the table. 'How are things with you?' he demanded abruptly.

'Marvellous!' Mary's voice held a lilt of enthusiasm.

Brett looked at her intently. 'Has Paul been to see you? He knows where you are.'

Mary sent him a baleful glare. 'Just don't mention that man's name to me. I know more about him now, and I don't want to talk about him. Nor do I want to see him again—ever. Do you understand?'

'Wise girl!' Brett applauded. 'Things are going smoothly at the motel?'

'They're fine. We've sent Aunt Laura to Auckland for a holiday and I've taken over the reception desk. I answer the phone, attend to the bookings and handle the cash. I go to the bank and—and do all sorts of things. I had no idea that meeting people could be such fun. I'm sure it's much more interesting than being stuck in an office all day.' The glance she sent Lisa was full of pity.

'I suppose Sally and Susan are kept busy,' Catherine murmured.

'Busy? They're flat out!' Mary told her. 'Guests who are leaving have to be out of their motels by ten in the morning, and then the rooms have to be prepared for the next people who'll occupy them. Susan attends to the changing of linen while Sally vacuums the carpets. Maggie cleans the basins, the shower floors and the cooking equipment in the self-contained units.'

'Who's Maggie?' Brett asked patiently.

Lisa drew a sharp breath as she guessed this person's identity.

'Maggie Simpson? She's an unmarried mother with a small boy,' Mary told him. 'She's been with them for a couple of years now. The little boy is dropped off at infants school while she does part-time work in the motel.' She fell silent as she buttered a bread roll, then added casually, 'If you must know, Paul Mason is the father of that same small boy. Maggie calls him Paul, and he's growing very like his father—the same light blue eyes and fair hair.'

'Maggie told you that?' Catherine asked sharply.

Mary laughed. 'Maggie tells everyone!'

Brett turned to Lisa. 'You knew about this girl Maggie—and the boy?'

She sent him a brief smile. 'Yes, I knew. It was this fact that knocked me for six and sent me running home to Auckland. It was something I—I just couldn't cope with.'

Brett's face turned stony. 'Why didn't you tell me about this girl and—Paul's son?'

She looked at him steadily. 'In the beginning it was because you wouldn't have believed me. You had your opinion concerning my reason for being here, and that was that. Later it became part of a bargain. He promised he wouldn't pester me if I promised I wouldn't mention it. He was trying to keep it a secret in this district.'

'Was he, indeed?' Brett's tone was grim.

Mary stood up to leave the table. 'Look, forget it, you two. It really doesn't matter now because—because——' She paused as a sudden flush deepened the colour of her cheeks. 'I might as well tell you, I've met somebody else. We dance every night.'

Catherine took notice at once. 'Who is he?' she

demanded, her face alert with interest as she regarded
Mary.

'You'll learn when you meet him,' Mary told her
teasingly. 'Now then, I need another suitcase and lots
more clothes.' She disappeared towards the boxroom.

Lisa felt as though a weight had been removed from
her shoulders. The situation between Mary and Paul
had been resolved, and now there was only her own
personal problem to combat. And the only way to do
this, she realised, was to complete *Mountain Memory*,
then pack her own bags.

During the next few days she worked with feverish
haste, being only vaguely aware of what went on
around her. She knew when the large shining steel
milk tanker passed along the road to call at the milking
shed, because she could almost set her watch by its
punctuality. And she knew that Dreaming Sam had
been put in a nearby field, because there were times
when she heard his bellowing roars that challenged
every other bull in the district. There was also the
occasional barking of dogs, but apart from these
sounds that were an integral echo of farm life, her
concentration remained unbroken.

And then came the day when she removed the cover
from Catherine's typewriter. Clean sheets of white
paper divided by a carbon paper were rolled in and her
fingers began tapping the keys. She heard Brett's
footsteps in the hall and she knew he had paused to
listen to the click-click, nor was she surprised when
the door was pushed open and he came into the room.

'So you've begun typing,' he remarked as he eyed
the machine.

'Yes. This is the beginning of the end.' She paused
to send him a mirthless smile.

He frowned. 'What do you mean?'

'I mean that the time has come when my days at
Lynton are now numbered.' She hated to admit it,
even to herself.

'And that'll be a damned big relief, I suppose?' he snapped.

'Not at all. I'll miss the sight of that peak out there, and—and the country way of life.'

'Country life? Huh! You've seen very little of that. You've been stuck in here all day and almost every day.'

'At least I can hear some of it,' Lisa defended. 'At times there's the bleat of a sheep or a bellow from Dreaming Sam. Has he settled down in his new home?'

'Sam settle down? That'll be the day! That bull's incorrigible. I now know why George Jones was so pleased to sell him. He's the best fence-destroyer in the district. He attacks posts and battens. He lunges and leans, pushes and shoves, and as the fence goes down he tramples over the wires. I'm waiting for the day when he meets Hercules at a fence-line.'

'Who, for heaven's sake, is Hercules?' queried Lisa.

'He's Mason's bull. Bulls are devils to fight.'

'Oh.' She fell silent, having no wish to continue a topic that included Paul. Then, feeling that something was expected of her, she said, 'Well, so long as it's Hercules he meets. Personally I've no wish to find myself face to face with him.'

'I don't think he'd hurt you. Sam's an intelligent animal. I'm sure he'd appreciate meeting a pretty girl.'

'Very funny! Obviously you must have your little joke.'

Brett looked at her curiously. 'Are you so very unaware of your own appearance?' he asked. 'To me you're quite beautiful.'

The words came as a shock. 'You're laughing at me!' she accused, turning her face away from him.

'I'm not, I promise you. I'm deadly serious. Can't you accept an olive branch when it's offered?' His fingers beneath her chin drew her face firmly back towards him.

She met his gaze wonderingly. Did he really consider her to be beautiful? His expression was sincere enough to cause a sudden radiant smile. Her eyes shone and her spirits began to float upwards as her former depression evaporated. At the same time she chided herself for being a pathetic idiot because he had only to look upon her kindly and she was ready to be moulded like clay in his hands.

In the silence during her thoughts an echo from Dreaming Sam floated into the room.

Brett frowned. 'He sounds as if he's rather close to the house. I must see John about more fencing wire.' Then, regarding her thoughtfully, 'You may be able to hear the sounds of the country, but as I said before, you haven't seen much of it. I doubt that you've even seen the milking shed.'

'Only from a distance. I caught a quick glimpse of it when we passed the Yates' house on the motorbike. It was the day you took me to examine the track—or perhaps you've forgotten.'

'Forgotten? Indeed I've a very clear recollection of that particular day.' He looked at her broodingly. 'In that case it's time you had a closer look at the heart of the farm. You can give yourself a break and come with me right now. Put on your rubber boots.'

'You're not slow to give orders,' Lisa remarked, standing up without haste and making a supreme effort to disguise her eagerness.

He shrugged. 'Okay, if you don't want to come——'

She capitulated at once. 'Yes, please, I'd like to see it.'

Moments later she had put on her warm jacket and rubber boots and had joined him outside in the cool fresh air. They crossed the yard and walked past the kennels where two Border Collies began leaping and barking with raucous agitation until they were silenced by a word of command.

'Quiet, Don—quiet, Dan!' Then to Lisa, 'They always tell me about it when I go past without letting them off the chain.'

He led her through gates and across the fields towards what appeared to be a round building surrounded by railed yards. Near it stood a large haybarn, and beyond it the Yates' house could be seen through the trees.

'It's a circular revolving shed,' Brett explained. 'It moves round slowly and smoothly on ball-bearings, very quietly, of course, otherwise it would upset the cows. It's a labour-saving device that makes it easy for one man to attend to many milking cups.'

Lisa looked at the steel pipes dividing the numerous compartments, then asked, 'How does he know when each cow is finished?'

'By the milk passing through a glass tube which enables him to see when each udder is empty. There's an overhead system of tubes to carry the milk away, but to understand the working of it you'd have to see it in action—that's if you're interested.'

She was awed by the efficiency of the plant. 'Of course I'm interested,' she exclaimed, delighting in the quiet companionship which now lay between them; nor did she find it difficult to understand Brett's pride in this modern milking shed. And then she was unable to resist a question. 'Is Paul's plant as up-to-date as this one?'

His brow darkened as he sent her a sharp glance. 'Not at present, but some day it might be,' he replied quietly.

'Do you mean he's thinking of installing one?'

'No. I've heard he's considering selling the place—no doubt in view of his plans to work in Auckland. If he decides to stay there it's unlikely he'd spend the money entailed in one of these costly sheds; however, the new owner might consider putting one in.'

His tone was abrupt, and she regretted her own

stupid curiosity which had probably given him the idea that Paul was never far from her thoughts—even if he no longer believed she had come to this district to find him.

But the suggestion that Paul might sell his farm had come as an unpleasant surprise. It meant he would be working near her home on a more permanent basis, which in turn meant she might have to cope with his unwelcome attentions towards herself. She gave a small inward sigh and decided to cross that particular bridge when she came to it, nor would she allow the fear of it to cloud these few precious moments with Brett.

During the days that followed this state of easy comradeship continued, although it was kept on a strictly platonic basis. Brett came to the library more frequently. He eyed the steadily growing number of completed pages, and as the pile grew higher, Lisa's hopes sank to a lower ebb.

It was an effort to keep her depression hidden, and each day found her forcing herself to put on a bright front while she worked her normal hours and took her usual walks out in the garden or along the drive. However, these outdoor breaks for exercise were now curtailed to fine days as winter was upon them.

The May of her arrival had slid into June, which in turn had glided into July. Taranaki's rainfall showed what it could do to swamp the countryside, and the mountain was almost continually shrouded in mist.

Even so the garden was not without colour. The bare branches of the japonica had broken out into a mass of brilliant red flowers, the red-hot pokers had sent up spikes of flaming torches, and early bulbs were making a splash of yellow beneath the kowhai tree in the corner of the garden. But Catherine's greatest joy at this particular time was a large round bed massed with anemones.

And then came a Tuesday which was to remain in

Lisa's mind as a black Tuesday, because it seemed to establish the fact that Brett would never feel more than brotherly affection towards herself. Later she was also to recall it as being the day of the bull.

The incident occurred after lunch when Catherine had left for her Country Women's Institute meeting. A reluctant sun had pierced the gloom of the winter day, making the opportunity for a short period outside too good to be missed. The golden rays called, so Lisa put on her jacket and rubber boots and left the house.

She walked down the drive and then tramped along the road. She breathed deeply, filling her lungs with the pure air until at last she turned to retrace her steps, hurrying now because she had walked further than she had intended. Nevertheless she felt refreshed, her mind cleared from the constant pressure of concentration.

But when she reached the drive a shock awaited her. As she turned from the road to cross the cattlestop the sight of Dreaming Sam brought her to an abrupt halt, her heart contracting with fear.

The bull stood in the centre of the driveway and appeared to be agitated, perhaps because he had found himself in a grassless area that was strange and not to his liking. Head down, he emitted low rumbling noises while he pawed the ground sufficiently to send up light clouds of dust.

Lisa stood petrified, staring at the dark head with its sharp horns, the large dark shoulders and fawn hindquarters. What should she do? There was no nearby fence for her to climb over, and if she turned back and ran along the road she felt sure the bull would follow her, jumping across the cattlestop without any trouble at all.

She looked about her frantically for a sign of Brett or John Yates, but neither of them could be seen. Nor would they know that Dreaming Sam had jumped over one of the garden fences and was now in the homestead enclosure.

But the main problem of the moment was her own course of action. She dared not walk past the animal, and she was still wondering what to do when he turned and faced her, his lowered head moving from side to side as he snorted with more rumbling sounds. She also knew that his dark eyes were watching her, and after further scrapings at the ground with a sharp hoof the bull took a few steps towards her.

Terror now gripped her as, hardly knowing where she was going, she shrieked and pushed through the shrubbery growing beneath the tree-ferns, then sped to the other side of the front garden. Her vague intention had been to give the bull a wide berth by circling the lawn to gain access to the house, but this tactic proved to be of little use, because the bull also crashed through the shrubbery. He stamped over the anemones, dug deep hoof-holes in the soft wet lawn, and again placed himself between Lisa and safety.

With this retreat cut off she did her best to hide from him by moving behind the camellia tree—and then her luck changed as the bright redness of the large japonica bush caught Dreaming Sam's attention. Head down, he charged into it, and there was a snapping and tearing of branches as his horns became entangled in the mass of light wood.

Lisa snatched at the opportunity to escape. She fled back to the drive and raced along its length to the house. By the time she reached the library she was white and shaking, and even the unexpected presence of Brett browsing over some of her typed pages did little to penetrate her agitated state of mind. She flung herself against him in a frenzy of agitation.

His arms went about her, supporting and holding her closely. 'Lisa, what the devil's the matter?'

'The bull—it's the bull!' she gasped breathlessly against his chest.

'Sam? You've been having words with Dreaming Sam?'

'I met him in the driveway. He—he gave me a ghastly fright!' She was still panting, nor was she able to stop shaking.

'Are you saying he's in the house grounds?' Brett's hand stroked her head, which now rested against his shoulder.

'At this moment he's—he's attending to that lovely japonica bush, and he's trampled over the bed of anemones. Catherine will be *furious*!' Reaction from her fright brought tears to her eyes and despite her efforts to control them she began to weep quietly.

Brett tipped her chin and looked down into her face. Her heart quickened a little as she felt sure he was about to kiss her, but such was not his intention. Instead he said, 'You're shedding tears for the flowers? They'll grow again, you know.'

She felt frustrated. 'I am *not* shedding tears for the flowers! No doubt you think I'm a fool, but I—I just can't seem to be able to stop them——' The words ended on a definite sob.

'Then have a good weep and get rid of the tension. Sam appears to have really upset you,' he added mildly.

'Upset me? That's an understatement!' Her voice rose in anger. 'You're taking very lightly the fact that I could have been gored to death!'

Brett laughed. 'By Sam? Rubbish! He's too polite.'

'That's what *you* think! He wasn't too polite to the japonica,' she snapped, glaring at him.

'Ah yes, but red is possibly something that irritates him. Normally he just likes to visit folk—a friendly sort of bloke.'

'Then let me tell you that even the quietest bull and I are—are—temperamentally incompatible!' she almost shouted.

'Is that a fact? In that case you'd never make a suitable wife for a dairy farmer, would you?' he teased.

'That possibility is as remote as—as the stars,' she hissed, trying to control her fury. And then a deeper turmoil began to manifest itself within her mind—an agitation built of frustration and bitter disappointment caused by the fact that Brett could take her ordeal so lightly. He didn't seem to care that she'd been scared almost out of her wits. He was really facetious about it.

*You'd never make a suitable wife for a dairy farmer*, he'd said.

And that statement summed up his whole attitude towards her. He'd looked her over just as he would a prize cow, and she'd been discarded. It was as simple as that. And instead of loving him she would be wiser to hate him—if she could—but which she could *not*. Well, it had been nice knowing him, and at least she knew for sure where she stood.

Suddenly she was in full control of her emotions. She dabbed at her eyes, blew her nose, then went to peer through the window. 'Okay, Brett,' she said smoothly. 'I'll now be interested to see you facing up to Dreaming Sam. He'll have to be got back into the paddock before he wrecks the entire garden.'

'That should be simple enough,' he replied easily.

'You'll just walk up to him?' Her eyes widened as she thought of the japonica bush.

'Not exactly. I'll have a little help,' he admitted.

'Help? You're expecting *me* to help you?' Her voice quavered.

'Not at all. But are you brave enough to come out and watch?' His amused tone held a challenge.

'Of course I am.' Pride forced the words from her lips.

But when they went outside he led her towards the back yard. 'Sam's in the front garden,' she pointed out patiently. 'He's not this way.'

'Ah, but the dogs are this way.' His patience equalled her own. 'Didn't I say I'd have help? I'll simply leave it to them. A job like this is right up their alley.'

Don and Dan leapt for joy when their chains were removed, but trotted quietly at Brett's heels as he and Lisa walked along the drive towards the front garden.

They found Dreaming Sam at the kowhai tree. His hoofs had trampled the yellow jonquils blooming at the base of the tree, and his horns tore at the bark as he rubbed his head against the trunk.

The dogs also saw the bull, but stood still, quivering with expectation as they awaited their orders which were not long in coming. Shrill whistles rang on the air and there was a flash of black fur as they raced towards the kowhai tree.

A sudden skirmish arose as the bull swung round to protect his hindquarters from the onslaught of biting jaws, but despite his roars, lowered head and sharp horns he was unable to cope with the snarling and barking from Don and Dan.

Bellowing loudly, he whirled round again. There was a loud screeching of strained fence wires as he crashed against the two top strands in an endeavour to escape the razor-sharp teeth snapping at his heels. The fence collapsed, and then, tail in the air, Dreaming Sam galloped across country with the two dogs following in high glee.

Brett stood watching for a short time before sending further shrill whistles ringing on the air. The two dogs stopped at once, then returned reluctantly, their wet tongues lolling from their mouths.

Lisa laughed as they paused to gaze longingly in the direction of the disappearing bull, then she followed Brett to the kennels where Don and Dan were again put on their chains.

'Do you think Sam will come back?' she asked nervously.

'I doubt it. He's now aware that the dogs are here

and he's not entirely stupid. In any case, he'll have to go back into the bull paddock.'

'Why was he allowed out of it?'

'Because it was short of feed. It needed to be given a rest to allow the grass to grow. I'll admit I've been far too lenient with him, but this time he's really blotted his copybook.'

The incident of the bull soon faded, and as the days passed life in the Lynton homestead continued on an even keel. At the same time *Mountain Memory* crept towards becoming a completed manuscript. Brett continued to watch its progress, coming in at times to relax in the fireside armchair while he read a few of the recently typed pages.

His presence was inclined to disturb Lisa, the main trouble lying in her own wayward thoughts. As her fingers tapped the keys her mind was apt to stray, wafting back to the precious moments when he had held her in his arms. But those unforgettable incidents now seemed to be far away in the past, and Brett's attitude of casual friendliness clearly indicated he had no desire to revive them.

There were also days when Catherine spent time in the library while making a thorough study of changes that had been made to what she still referred to as her life's work. 'This has been a tremendous lesson to me,' she admitted. 'Such economy of words!'

'It comes with practice,' Lisa promised her reassuringly. 'After all, this is your first book. You'll do better next time.'

Catherine sent her a sidelong glance. 'Next time. Ah yes, I've been meaning to talk to you about this next book on the early women—but first let me ask you a question. Have you enjoyed being here, or has it been an irksome bore?'

'A bore? Certainly not! I've loved it.'

'You haven't missed the city lights?'

'Oh no. I'm beginning to suspect I'm a country girl

at heart.' Lisa looked through the window, her blue eyes holding a wistful expression. 'Or perhaps it's that old mountain magic.'

Catherine took a deep breath. 'In that case I'll make a suggestion that's been simmering in my mind. What would you say to doing the next book with me?'

'You mean we'd do it here—at Lynton, together?'

'Yes. I'll see if I can arrange it with Gordon.'

Lisa shook her head dubiously. 'I don't think he'd agree to it for one moment. Didn't he say he wanted me back in the office as soon as possible? I'm sure he'll tell you to write it yourself and then send it in for assessment. Besides——' She hesitated, then fell silent.

'Yes? Besides what?' The hazel eyes had taken on a piercing glint that seemed to bore into Lisa.

'Besides, I—I rather suspect that Brett thinks it's time I was on my way home,' said Lisa in a low voice.

'Nonsense! What gives you that silly idea?'

'Perhaps it's because he's given no intimation that he'd like me to stay. I'm sure he thinks I've been here for long enough.'

'Then he's a fool,' Catherine snapped impatiently. 'Really, I'd have thought——' She fell silent.

'Yes? You'd have thought what?' Lisa sat back in her chair and sent Catherine a direct questioning stare.

'If you must know the truth, my dear, I've been hoping that you and Brett could get together, that you'd make a match of it. I took a fancy to you when we first met in Gordon's office, and as I began to know you better I thought, ah, this is the girl for Brett.'

Lisa was unable to look at her. 'That's very sweet of you, Catherine,' she murmured.

'I might as well be honest—it was my prime reason for wanting you to edit the book here at Lynton. I felt sure that if I could get the pair of you together——'

'But it hasn't worked. I'm afraid Brett looks upon

me as—as nothing more than a—a younger sister. I can assure you he's not even remotely in love with me.'

'Then he's a damned fool,' Catherine said with some force. 'He's as blind as a bat—far too blind to see a diamond when it's shoved right under his nose.' She looked at Lisa shrewdly, then appeared to choose her words with care. 'But what about you? Is it possible you could have fallen in love with Brett?'

Lisa felt her colour rising. It would be useless to lie to Catherine, she decided, so she remained silent.

'Ah, I thought so,' Catherine said quietly. 'You silence tells me all I need to know. If the answer had been no you'd have told me so quite definitely and without hesitation. In the meantime, my dear, I hope you'll give some serious thought to doing the next book with me.'

Lisa gave a wan smile. 'It's very tempting, but I'm sure your brother would never agree. He'll tell you I've been away from the office for far too long as it is.'

'You leave Gordon to me,' said Catherine with determination.

During her next walk along the road Lisa pondered the proposition, but discarded it almost immediately. Not for one moment could she imagine Gordon Bishop conceding to Catherine's wishes, but apart from that the project would merely prolong her own agony of experiencing Brett's casual attitude towards herself.

But life had to go on and the time had come for her to take a firm grip on her own emotions as well as the situation. The day was approaching when she must return to work in the Auckland office. She would have to accept the state of living without the nearness of Brett and of not being able to see him every day, hear his voice or listen for the sound of his step. Her life, she knew, would never be the same again.

And then she realised she had walked further than

usual, having been so deep in thought she had passed the place where she normally turned to retrace her steps. Pausing to stare about her, she could see the house she knew belonged to Paul, and even as she stared at it two men emerged and stood talking. One was Paul, while the other was easily recognisable as Brett. They appeared to be on friendly terms as they walked towards Paul's milking shed.

Lisa turned her back and hurried towards home, because she had no wish for Brett to see her. He might imagine she had been watching his movements, or worse still, coming to visit Paul. However, she was not slow to realise that his association with his neighbour seemed to be amicable, and it was also obvious that he held no animosity towards Paul because of the latter's interest in herself.

Nevertheless, she was unprepared for the surprise that awaited her that evening.

# CHAPTER TEN

The surprise came when they were relaxing after the evening meal. The dishes had been rinsed and stacked into the dishwasher, and a tray bearing a coffee pot and small cups had been carried into the lounge.

Lisa noticed that Brett was thoughtfully silent as he sipped his coffee. She was vitally conscious of his presence, and from the corner of her eye she saw him put his cup on the small table beside him, unfold his long legs and cross the room to the low wood cupboard set beside the fireplace.

She watched as he bent to place several short pine logs on the flames, but was unprepared for what almost amounted to an attack when he turned to face her. Standing with his back to the blaze, he looked at her accusingly, yet when he spoke his voice was deceptively casual.

'I saw you on the road today. Do you always walk as far as the entrance to Paul's drive?'

She shook her head. 'It's the first time I've been near it. Does it matter how far I walk?' So he *had* seen her.

'Not at all. Did you intend making a visit, then changed your mind when you saw us in the field?'

'Certainly not! Your imagination is running away with you. I'll admit I walked further than usual today, but that was because the constant rain has prevented my normal short walks!'

Catherine spoke to Brett. 'Are you saying you were with Paul? I'm glad Mary's episode with him hasn't made you enemies. I don't like quarrels between neighbours.'

Brett gave a short laugh. 'It won't make much

difference as far as Paul is concerned. He won't be here, because he's sold his farm.'

Catherine's jaw dropped slightly. 'Sold his farm? I wonder who's bought it?'

'There's no need to wonder. I've bought it,' announced Brett as though it was the most natural thing to have done.

Catherine put her coffee cup down with care, then sat erect in her chair. '*You?* Did you say you've bought Paul's farm?'

'Your hearing is as good as ever, Cathy dear.'

She digested the information in silence, then added, 'You'll keep on his share-milker?'

'Of course. He'll be made a manager and put on a higher salary.'

'I must say I'm surprised,' said Catherine in a bemused tone. 'I can't understand why Paul should want to sell his farm.'

'I think the answer lies in his desire to live on Auckland's North Shore,' Brett replied, with an edge to his voice and his eyes on Lisa's face. 'He's also wise enough to know he can't live so far away from such a valuable asset and still keep his eye on it. No doubt he'll invest his money elsewhere.'

'He's a fool,' Catherine snapped. 'His money is safer invested in land.' She turned to Lisa. 'What do you think?'

Lisa shook her head vaguely, lost for words. Secretly she was appalled by this turn of events which seemed to give a permanence to Paul's move to the North Shore, but fortunately there was no need to find an answer, because Catherine wanted more details.

'How did it happen so quickly?' the latter demanded. 'These land sales usually take ages, what with valuations and so forth——'

'Naturally a valuation was made,' Brett assured her easily. 'However, Paul wanted the sale completed as rapidly as possible so that he could get himself settled in Auckland. He appears to have a reason for wanting to be there quite soon.' His eyes held a cool glint as they rested on Lisa.

She controlled the angry words that rose to her lips and listened as Brett continued to give further information.

'He told me the price he was asking and I said I'd give it to him. Of course it included the stock. The papers have already been signed in the solicitor's office.'

Lisa felt slightly stunned. Even her limited knowledge told her that a dairy farm plus a pedigree herd must have cost the earth. She also knew that Brett was watching for her reaction to the news, and only with an effort did she manage to say casually, 'Now I know why you were so sure the next owner of Paul's property would alter the milking shed to a circular revolving unit.'

Little was said during the remainder of the evening. The television offered entertainment which hardly registered in Lisa's mind as she fought her steadily growing dejection. She peeped at Catherine and noticed that she frowned as she watched the programme, while Brett's face appeared to be expressionless. No doubt he was mentally planning further changes to his new property.

He seemed to have made it so easy for Paul to wind up his affairs in this district and to make his move to Auckland, she thought bitterly. He *knew* that Paul had amorous intentions towards herself, yet it almost seemed as though she was being handed to him on a dish! An irritating prickle of tears made her blink rapidly, and within a short time she made her excuses and went to bed where she wept into the pillow.

After that evening the days seemed to flit past with a speed that was frightening. Lisa threw herself into completing the manuscript while Catherine continued to read and approve its new form. Photographs which had been stored in a large flat box were now brought out and examined for inclusion, their captions and places in the manuscript also being attended to.

'What about the index?' asked Catherine, as though grasping at a straw that could possibly keep Lisa at Lynton for a few more days.

'Your brother employs a girl who does all our index work,' Lisa explained. 'He won't expect me to stay here to do it.'

'I'll hate to see you leave here,' Catherine almost wailed. 'I could bang Brett's head against the wall.'

'Why?' Brett's voice rasped from the doorway. 'What have I done to bring on this state of rage?'

Catherine spun round and glared at him. 'It's what you *haven't* done that riles me!' Her face slightly flushed, she swept past him and left the room.

'What's all this about?' he snapped at Lisa.

'How would I know?' she retorted, brushing the question aside.

'From the little I heard it appeared to have something to do with your leaving this place.'

'Which will take place during the next couple of days,' Lisa informed him coolly. 'I shall type a list of the photographs, and then I'll pack my bags.'

'And hurry home to Paul,' Brett added calmly.

Her eyes were shadowed as she looked at him steadily. 'I have a strong feeling you'd like to see me do just that,' she said.

'You don't appear to understand that I want to know the *best* is happening for you, Lisa.' His low voice held sincerity.

With equal sincerity she said, 'If Catherine bangs your head against the wall I hope I'm there to help her.'

He looked at her in silence for several moments before he said, 'In some way I seem to be doing the wrong thing. Doesn't it occur to you that, deep down, you might still love Paul? You told me you expected to get engaged, so I consider you should be given the opportunity to make sure of your true feelings towards him. You'll be able to do that.'

She gave a sigh of utter weariness that was born of frustration. 'I did that a long time ago, Brett.'

'But don't you *see*, Lisa? I want you to be sure—*absolutely sure.*'

She looked at him sadly. 'I'm afraid there's nothing more to be said, Brett.' Turning away from him, she rolled a blank sheet into the typewriter, then began tapping out a list of the photographs that would illustrate Catherine's book. Nor did she look at him again, although she knew when he left the room.

She worked frantically for the rest of the day, her mind delierately shutting out the image of Brett. By evening the editing of *Mountain Memory* was complete, with the chapters and photographs neatly packed into a small case.

As she closed the lid a slight lump rose to Lisa's throat, not because the work on the manuscript was finished, but because her days at Lynton were now at an end. She left the library hastily and went to drag her own suitcase from the boxroom, and as she carried it through the hall she met Brett.

His dark brows arched as he regarded the case. 'Does this mean you've actually finished?'

She nodded. 'The list of photos took less time than I expected.'

'Then you're packing up to leave?'

'Yes. Catherine will be driving me to New Plymouth tomorrow, and I'll catch a plane from there to Auckland.' Then, fearing that her inner emotions could be revealed, she hurried towards her bedroom.

But next morning it wasn't Catherine's car that waited at the back door; it was Brett's silver-grey Holden. He was dressed in well-cut clothes for town, and as he put her cases in the boot he said, 'I've decided to make sure you catch the plane.'

The words were accompanied by a smile and spoken jokingly, nevertheless they came as tiny stab wounds. However, she managed to send him a level glance and to say evenly, 'Don't worry, I'll be on it. I had no idea you were so anxious to be rid of me.'

He gripped her shoulders, stared into her face and gave her a slight shaking. 'You really believe that?'

Lisa returned his stare defiantly. 'You've made it clear enough.'

His hands left her shoulders to put cases for Catherine and himself beside her own.

Looking at them, she said, 'You'll be staying in New Plymouth?'

'Yes, for a couple of days. Catherine intends to spend time at the public library and I have a couple of men to interview. I'll need extra staff for the new place. They both live just out of New Plymouth, so I'll see them tomorrow.'

She was surprised. 'Why don't they come to you to be interviewed?'

'Because I want to meet their wives and observe the state of their present homes.'

'My goodness, you're very thorough!' she commented.

'Is that something you're only just learning?' drawled Brett.

Rain poured during the drive to New Plymouth, soaking the already drenched countryside. Visibility was poor, and as she sat in the back seat of the Holden Lisa gazed to where the mountain stood completely hidden by a blanket of dense clouds. The thoughts running through her head were anything but happy.

You should be ashamed of yourself, Taranaki, she chided silently. You called me here, and I'll bet it was you who made me fall in love—and now that I'm leaving you haven't the grace to show your face, you rotten great heap!

But the next instant her irritation had turned

towards herself. Stupid idiot, she thought. The mountain's magic couldn't stretch that far. It was Brett himself who made me start loving him—and who doesn't want me. Isn't he even making sure I get on the plane?

But this did not happen as quickly as expected. Rain, low cloud and mist rolling in from the sea all combined to close the New Plymouth airport, and Lisa had no option but to accompany Brett and Catherine to the motel owned by their relatives.

The two sisters, Susan and Sally, greeted them with delight, but explained to Catherine that their mother had extended her holiday by flying from Auckland to Fiji. They ushered them into a well-appointed sea-front unit with two double bedrooms, and while Lisa and Catherine shared one, Brett settled himself into the other.

They had a light lunch from the hamper prepared by Catherine, who then asked to be driven to the public library. Turning to Brett, she said, 'I know I can rely on you to take care of Lisa.'

'Thank you for the confidence.' His tone was dry, his face inscrutable, nor did he glance at either of them.

Lisa's heart sank as she sensed his reluctance, but she forced a smile as she said, 'Please don't worry about me. If the rain stops I'll go for a walk.

A short time later they drove Catherine to the library, and as she left the car she declared she would find her own way home when she was ready. They watched as she entered the building, then Brett turned to Lisa, his eyes holding a strange brooding expression.

'Well, what now? What would you like to do?' he asked abruptly.

Startled, she looked at him blankly. 'I—I don't know. The weather is against such places as the parks or—or the beaches.' She turned away from him. Why on earth had she mentioned the *beach*? It could only remind him of their previous episode on the sands that were as black as the shores encircling New Plymouth.

What was it he'd said on that occasion? *You have no need to fear for any further cause for complain from me.* How could she tell him that she longed for him to want her, that it wouldn't be cause for complaint?

He cut into her thoughts with an abrupt remark. 'We'll visit the Cottage Museum. It's a good place for a wet day.'

'Yes, that would be interesting.' Her smile hid her deep disappointment as she realised the Cottage Museum would have other people in it, whereas he could have taken her to a more secluded place. But apparently he had no wish to do so, not even on their last day together.

They left the car in a nearby parking area and went into the cottage, which immediately enveloped them in an atmosphere of the past. Lisa was drawn towards the hearth of the wide open fireplace where heavy black cast-iron kettles, pots and oval boilers offered mute evidence of the type of cooking utensils used in earlier days.

Brett pointed to a round squat object that stood on three legs. 'That's a camp oven,' he told her. 'It stands on the hot embers with more embers being piled on top of the lid. Catherine has one. If ever you come again you must ask her for a demonstration.'

*If ever I come again.* The words gave her a lift, making her realise that at least he thought she *might* come again. They had the effect of making her feel happier, and as they slowly examined each exhibit in the cottage she became aware that relations between them had reached the stage of being pleasantly amicable.

This state of easy friendship remained with them for the rest of the evening. Susan and Sally insisted that they all have dinner together, and during the meal

Lisa was aware that Brett's eyes were constantly straying towards her. She knew she looked nice, because she had changed into her eye-catching dress of fine red wool and had taken extra care with her make-up.

Nor was it easy to control her suppressed excitement when Brett later led her towards the area set aside for dancing. The floors of the combined rooms had been attended to, and coloured lights threw a soft mystic glow over the numerous indoor plants set between seats arranged round the walls.

Other couples staying in the motel were there before them, moving to the haunting melody of a slow waltz, and as he took her in his arms Lisa feared he might become aware of the mad thudding of her heart.

'Do you know you're very beautiful tonight, Lisa?' he murmured, his chin resting against her forehead.

'Thank you—you're looking rather smart yourself. This is a lovely jacket.' She knew it was an inane remark and not at all what she wanted to say, but her mind was in a whirl as his arm held her against him and she felt the sinuous movement of his body sway in rhythm against her own.

'I'm beginning to wonder why the hell I'm allowing you to go home,' he muttered huskily.

Her head almost swam. 'Oh? You had—something in mind?' she dared to ask hopefully, then her pulses quickened as she waited for the words she longed to hear.

He was silent, his only answer being to place both arms about her body and to hold her even closer to his breast as they danced.

Still she waited patiently. Brett never did things in a hurry, she realised, and the words would be all the sweeter when they came.

Was it possible that he *did* love her and was about to admit it at last? But memory of having previously reached this point niggled at her. For instance, there had been those moments on the beach when she had felt so sure he had been about to tell her—yet they had ended in anticlimax. However, she was conscious of something entirely different about these particular moments.

The tempo of the music quickened to swing into the whirl of an old-fashioned waltz which sent them spinning round and round as he crushed her against his heart. His cheek against her forehead, she felt herself to be almost floating up into the clouds while her feet seemed to be hardly touching the floor.

She also knew they were drawing glances from other people in the room, and she caught a glimpse of Mary watching them wide-eyed from the doorway where she stood beside a man. But Lisa didn't care. Sooner or later Mary would guess that Brett loved her and that they were about to become engaged. Or was this mere wishful thinking? she was jolted into asking herself.

The music came to an abrupt end. Brett stood gazing down into her upturned face, a dazed expression in his eyes as though he had been dragged back to earth without warning. His arms were still about her as he said, 'Lisa—Lisa, that was wonderful! You're a great little dancer—why the devil haven't I taken you dancing before?'

'I loved it, Brett—let's dance some more.' Her eyes shone.

And then the spell was completely shattered by Mary's voice as she crossed the floor followed by the man who was with her.

'Hey, break it up, you two—you look as if you're both in a trance!' Her face was glowing and her voice gay as she made the introductions. 'Brett, this is Peter Stevens—Peter, I want you to meet my brother Brett and—and our friend Lisa Longmore.'

The two men shook hands, but for Lisa the magic atmosphere had been swept away by Mary and her new boy-friend. She had no option but to follow them to the lounge where Brett and Peter fell into conversation, seeking mutual interests and getting to know each other. And worse still, Peter's hobby was mountain-climbing.

Catherine was there too, her sharp eyes taking in every detail of Peter Stevens while plying him with subtle questions that would tell her whether or not he was a 'suitable' young man for Mary.

As far as Lisa was concerned the evening had reached a state of anticlimax. She felt sick with disappointment, and, frustrated, she went to bed early. And there she shed tears into the pillow, until common sense prevailed and she began to think a little more clearly.

How could she expect Brett to reveal his feelings with all those other people around them—or even whisper that he loved her? The dance floor had not been the place for such a declaration. And there was still tomorrow morning before she was due to catch the plane—weather permitting, of course.

But next morning the sky had cleared, the airport was open, yet of Brett there was no sign.

Catherine said, 'He's driven into the country to interview one of his prospective employees. I'm sure he'll be back in time to take us to the airport.' Nevertheless she looked anxious.

He was back in time, but with little to spare. Lisa's suitcases were dumped hurriedly into the boot of the Holden, and although the airport was only a short distance away there was need for speed.

Lisa sat in the back seat with Catherine's flow of chatter wafting over her head. It was mainly about Mary and Peter, who were the last people she happened to be interested in during those last crucial moments with Brett.

But what was the use? Obviously he didn't love her, and she had been lost in a pipe dream of her own making.

A short time later she sat in the plane waiting for take-off. She was fighting her tears and as she peered through the window she had a view of the mountain's peak peeping through the clouds.

You old fool! she muttered at it in silent disgust. You and your magic! It's a load of rubbish and nothing more.

On Monday morning Lisa walked into Gordon Bishop's office and put the manuscript and photos on his desk.

The sight of her brought a beam of delight to his face. 'Ah, you're back! I was really afraid——' He flicked a rapid glance towards her left hand.

Her blue eyes, slightly shadowed, met his squarely. 'Yes? You were saying you were afraid. Of what, may I ask?'

'I feared that Brett would have had something to say about your returning to Auckland,' he admitted abruptly.

'If he had anything to say he kept it to himself,' said Lisa, unaware of the doleful note in her voice.

His eyes narrowed slightly as he looked at her. 'You're all right? You're looking very pale. You're not your usual self.'

'I'm quite well, thank you.' She wasn't, but she had no intention of going into details. She had hardly slept and found difficulty in swallowing her food, but she told herself she'd get over it.

Gordon Bishop examined the manuscript, checking the number of pages. 'This appears to be a more reasonable size. Did you have much trouble with Catherine when you began cutting it down?'

'None at all. She's a darling.'

'And her stepson—is he also a darling?' The question came casually, but his eyes had a shrewd look within their depths.

Lisa remained cool, refusing to be needled into an

admission of any sort. 'Brett? He's very busy. He's recently bought a new property—and Mary is about to become engaged.' She passed off the information as family news.

'Hmm. Well, your office is waiting for you, and there's this thing that's just come in. You can give it your attention.' He handed her a new manuscript.

Lisa took it gratefully, thankful to see that it was about Westland in the South Island and had nothing at all to do with Taranaki. It would help clear that place from her mind, and, most important of all, it would stop Brett's face from dancing before her eyes. Or so she hoped.

But it didn't. Thought of him continued to invade her mind until her work began to be affected from lack of concentration.

Gordon Bishop frowned as he said, 'What the devil's the matter with you, Lisa? I've never known you make so many typing errors, to say nothing of some of these spelling mistakes. Your mind's not on your work, my girl. You'd better pull your socks up.'

The reprimand jarred but did little to help matters, although she did her best to keep her eyes open for careless errors. And as the days passed she began to lose weight, the shadows about her eyes deepened, and the fine bone structure of her face became more prominent. The change made her look mature yet more beautiful.

'Are you dieting?' Gordon snapped at her when she'd been back at work for a month.

Lisa shook her head and hurried from his office, conscious that her work was still suffering in various places.

Coupled with these problems was the even more irritating one of Paul Mason. On arrival at his new job he had been placed in the firm's Auckland office rather than on the North Shore, and from the moment of her return he had made a nuisance of himself.

Each day when she left the office for lunch she found him waiting for her at the foot of the stairs. When she changed her lunch hour he searched until he found her in one of the nearby restaurants. At the end of each day he was there, pleading to be allowed to drive her home, but this she refused and hurried away to catch the bus that would take her to the North Shore.

'I'm not giving up, Lisa,' he told her stubbornly on one occasion. 'I'll wear you down until you come back to me.'

'So much for your promise to leave me alone!' she exclaimed angrily.

'Oh, *that*. You can forget it. Things have changed.'

'You're wasting your time, Paul,' she told him. 'And please don't send more flowers to the office. You might as well know I give them to other members of the staff.'

Matters became worse when he began making visits to her office. Brief as these calls were, she was terrified Gordon would discover him wasting her time, and then there would be a further reprimand. Nor did he heed her pleas when she asked him to stay away.

And then the day came when he walked into her room, closed the door and stood grinning at her. 'Hi there, gorgeous—you're coming out with me tonight, and I won't take no for an answer.'

Lisa looked at him wearily. 'Oh? Who says so?'

'I say so. Come on, Lisa—there's a staff dinner party and I must have a partner. Surely you could do me the favour——'

'I'm sorry, Paul, you'll have to find somebody else. I'm feeling rather tired these days.' The thought of a dinner party when she could hardly eat the food placed before her at home made her feel ill. At the same time she realised that a social outing would probably help her—but not with Paul. She couldn't endure the thought of going out with Paul.

He looked at her sceptically. 'Tired? You? That's a weak excuse. You've always been full of energy.'

'Well, I'm not now. Nor am I going out with you. Please, Paul, would you just leave me alone?' Her voice held a ring of desperation that echoed her state of mind.

His face took on a mutinous expression. 'For Pete's sake, snap out of it, Lisa—it's time you got over this stupidity of shutting me out in the cold! We've had good times before and we can have them again, if only you'd come to your senses.'

'I'm sorry, Paul, I don't intend to argue with you.' She left her desk to cross the room and open the door. 'Now, will you please go?' Her voice had become icy.

'No, I'll be damned if I will!'

A few strides took him to her and the next moment she was struggling against the strength of his arms. She gasped, hammering at his chest with clenched fists, but he only laughed at her weak efforts. Even so she was able to shout and call for help.

To her relief the tussle was brief, because an unexpected force from behind Paul grabbed him by the collar and thrust him out into the passage that ran between the various offices. But it wasn't Gordon Bishop who had come to her aid—it was Brett who now stood scowling at Paul.

'Can't you latch on to the fact that the lady doesn't want you?' he rasped.

Paul glared at him. 'Oh, so you're the reason she won't come out with me tonight! I might've known you'd be in the picture somewhere. Okay, goodbye, Lisa,' he muttered as he made a hasty exit towards the stairs and past faces now peeping from other doors.

Brett closed the door of Lisa's office and stood leaning against it, his arms folded across his chest as he drank in every detail of her appearance.

She returned his gaze in silence, hardly daring to believe he was actually standing before her, and fearing he might vanish like a puff of smoke. 'Thank you for arriving at such a critical time,' she said at last. Her eyes, glowing with pleasure, looked larger than usual. 'Is Catherine with you?'

He shook his head. 'No. I came alone.'

'Oh.' She felt lost for words. 'She's well?'

'Yes. I've left her in New Plymouth while I'm making this trip to Auckland.' His eyes seemed to be penetrating every part of her.

'You have business here?' Then as he nodded she added softly, 'I'm glad you've—you've found time to come and see me.'

'I'm doing more than that. I've come to take you home.'

Her jaw dropped slightly. 'I—I don't understand——'

'I've come to ask you to marry me. I love you very much, Lisa.'

She looked at him in wonderment. Was she hearing correctly? 'I—I beg your pardon? I almost thought you said——'

'You heard me, Lisa. I said I'm asking you to marry me.'

A gasp escaped her and she took an involuntary step towards him, but he held up a restraining hand.

'No, just stay over there. I want you to think about it clearly, rather than in the warmth of an embrace, though God knows I'm longing to hold you.'

Her eyes shone. 'I don't have to think about it, Brett, I've known the answer for ages. Of course I'll marry you—I—I thought you'd never ask!'

They met halfway across the room and she was in his arms, his lips on hers in a kiss that spoke of a love that would be everlasting. His hands ran possessively over her body and she sighed with utter contentment as he held her against him.

'You're thinner,' he said, looking at her with concern. 'Why have you lost weight?'

She ignored the question by asking another. Somehow it was important for her to know the answer. 'Brett, have you only just discovered you love me?'

He shook his head. 'Of course not, my darling. I suspected it from the first moment of your arrival. It took time for me to admit to what had struck me—and then I was constantly bedevilled by nagging fears.'

She rested against him, her arms about his waist as she waited to hear that these fears had now been swept from his mind.

'You'll recall that at first I suspected you'd come in search of Paul?'

Lisa gave a shaky laugh. 'How could I forget?'

'I'd no sooner cleared my mind on that point than I woke up to the fact that Catherine had been up to her old matchmaking tactics. At first I was in a rage, but it soon passed because yet another fear had raised its head.'

She looked up at him, her eyes full of questions. 'What else could there have been?'

'The fear that perhaps you were beginning to realise that it was Paul you really loved. I thought that if you returned to Auckland without any commitment to me you'd be given a fair chance to be sure about it.'

'You've no idea how much misery you put me through!' she whispered against his chest.

'I was trying to take the best course for you, my dearest. I decided to give you three months.'

'Three months? But it's not yet six weeks!'

'No. The moment you stepped aboard that plane I knew I couldn't live without you. Nor could I wait three months. Darling Lisa, how soon can we be married?' His voice was pleading.

Her head was spinning with joy. 'As soon as—as possible. Would you believe I can almost hear that old mountain calling?'

Brett laughed, then crushed her to him. 'He'll have

to keep on calling until we've had our honeymoon. How about somewhere overseas?' He bent his head to kiss her with a deep hunger that sent her entire being up into the clouds.

But suddenly she came back to earth as Gordon Bishop's voice spoke from behind them. He had come in unheard and now stood watching them with an amused glint in his eyes. 'Honeymoon overseas, eh? I knew I should have had my head examined before allowing Lisa to go to Lynton—any fool could have told me I'd lose her! Dammit, it's all Catherine's fault. Well, I suppose I'd better congratulate you, Brett.'

As they shook hands Brett said, 'You can give Lisa the rest of the day off. I'm taking her shopping in Queen Street.'

'Ah, to the jewellery shops, no doubt?'

'Correct.' Brett took Lisa's arm. 'Come along, my darling—you're about to choose your engagement ring!'

Her head was still in a whirl when, less than an hour later, a large sapphire encircled by diamonds was slipped on to her finger. Everything had happened so unexpectedly, and as she gazed at its brilliance she knew that the first era of her existence on this earth was ending, while a new life with Brett was about to begin.

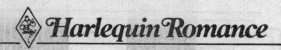

# Harlequin Romance

## Coming Next Month

**2797 BOSS OF YARRAKINA Valerie Parv**
A sham engagement for the sake of her aunt's health is one
thing; marriage, quite another. And Joselin goes out of her way
to avoid tying the knot with the boss of Yarrakina—only to
discover he truly is the man for her.

**2798 THE LAST BARRIER Edwina Shore**
In Scotland, a young woman who's still overwhelmed by the
accident that killed her fiancé, resists when her heart goes out
to a young orphan and to the boy's disturbing uncle.

**2799 ONE LIFE AT A TIME Natalie Spark**
The search is over, but her problems are just beginning. She's
found the man she fell in love with three years ago—the man
who'd lost his memory. Only he seems to have forgotten her.

**2800 SO NEAR, SO FAR Jessica Steele**
A secretary's new boss lectures her about her reputation with
men and insists he won't be taken in by her wiles. Now how
can she make him like her without confirming his worst
suspicions?

**2801 AUTUMN IN APRIL Essie Summers**
The nerve of the man! She and his grandfather had discussed
love. Not money. The undying love the older man had felt for
her grandmother—the kind of love Matthieu obviously didn't
understand.

**2802 BREAKING FREE Marcella Thompson**
Admittedly, this city slicker knows nothing about farming. But
she intends to fulfill her poultry contract with Clear Creeks
Farm in Arkansas—if only to show the arrogant owner what
she's made of.

Available in November wherever paperback books are sold,
or through Harlequin Reader Service.

In the U.S.
P.O. Box 1397
Buffalo, N.Y.
14240-1397

In Canada
P.O. Box 2800, Postal Station A
5170 Yonge Street
Willowdale, Ontario M2N 6J3

# Here's how to get this special offer from Harlequin!

✂ October
BETTY NEELS
TREASURY EDITION
COUPON

## As simple as 1...2...3!

1. Each month, save one Treasury Edition coupon from your favorite Romance or Presents novel.
2. In four months you'll have saved four Treasury Edition coupons (only one coupon per month allowed).
3. Then all you have to do is fill out and return the order form provided, along with the four Treasury Edition coupons required and $2.95 for postage and handling.